THE

ORANGE GIRL OF VENICE.

A ROMANCE.

LONDON:

PUBLISHED BY E. LLOYD, 12, SALISBURY-SQUARE,
FLEET-STREET.

THE ORANGE GIRL
OF VENICE

CHAPTER I.

THE STUDENT.

In a low vaulted chamber, in the upper story of a humble building, situated in a disreputable section of the far-famed queen of the Adriatic, sat a youth of some three and twenty years. A low, broad, cross-legged table was before him, on which, in careless disorder, some ten or twenty volumes, bound in parchment, and ornamented with metal clasps, were scattered. Sheets of unstained parchment lay here and there, while directly before him was a sheet half filled with annota-

No. 1.

tions, dates, &c., apparently for reference. A saucer of brass, containing a dark liquid, rested within a few inches of the spotted parchment, while a long grey quill, cut at the tip, and stained with writing fluid, lay on the edge of the table, as if just put down. The youth leaned backward in his low-seated but high-backed chair, his right hand supporting his pale, high brow, while his left hung listlessly over he cross-piece of his chair. The features of the youth were more of the feminine hen of the masculine cast, the forehead being high and pale, the eye dark, lustrous yet soft and melting, the cheek pale, the eye arching, the nose small, and with but a slight show of nostrils; the lip slight; and the chin small but pointed. He wore a small, silky mustache, and a slight pointed tuft adorned his chin. His hair was dark and redundant, and fell in long, wavy curls on his narrow shoulders. He wore a tunic of ordinary grey cloth, square at the neck, and bordered with dark velvet. His pantaloons, fitting tightly to the skin, were of a blue colour, but somewhat faded by constant use. His shoes were of a russet hue, and ornamented with rosettes of the same colour.

The apartment was small, containing one window only, through which the moonlight entered, and fell upon a low, rude couch in a corner, which gave evidence of the lateness of the hour when its master rose. Hanging on a peg, over the couch was a cross-hilted sword, sheathed in a scabbard of bright yellow metal, while a, belt of dark velvet hung down its side. A slouched cap of grey stuff, with a full, jetty plume, hung against the wall, a short distance from the sword, while a mantle of dark cloth rested beside it. The rest of the apartment was chillingly bare.

The student appeared rapt in meditation, his eye falling vacantly upon the parchment before him. A small three-cornered lamp burnt dimly beside the saucer, giving to his countenance the appearance of one overworked with midnight toil.

A knock at his chamber door roused him from thought, and, in a deep stern voice, as he turned slightly round in his chair, he bade the knocker enter.

The door opened, and a tall, majestic person, enveloped in a mantle of dark and glossy velvet, of the finest texture, entered the apartment. A slouched cap, of the same material as his mantle, surmounted by a cluster of raven plumes, adorned his head. He wore mustachios, and his bold chin was hid beneath a thick, jetty beard. His eyes was large, black, and piercing as an eagle's; his forehead was high and massive, and there was an expression of sternness and resolution about his broad nostrils and firm upper lip, calculated to strike a beholder with awe.

On perceiving the garb and rank of his visitor, the student sprang hastily from his seat, and offered it to the stranger. The latter took it in silence, and motioned the student to be also seated.

"Thou art called Calvari, the scribe, art thou not?" said the stranger.

"I am, my lord," replied the student, bowing in surprise.

"Thou dealest in ancient and modern lore, dost thou not?"

"A little, my lord."

"Canst translate me this?" said the stranger, drawing from his girdle a letter and handing it to the student.

"I will try, my lord," replied the student, advancing towards the lamp, and opening the parchment.

The face of the student grew pale, as he glanced at the characters traced on the page.

"Thy cheek blushes," observed the stranger, resting his sharp eye upon the student.

"Doth it, my lord?" said the student, falteringly.

"Ay, it doth. The meaning of't?"

"Take back the parchment, my lord," said the student, with increased agitation. "I—I—dare not translate its language!"

"Dare not!" exclaimed the other, ironically. "What fearest thou?"

"Death!" answered the student, holding the parchment towards the stranger.

"Ha! is it so?" cried the latter, starting up, and seizing the document. "Lies the wind that way?" he added in irony, glancing with a curled lip and contemptuous eye at the pale student. "Go to, I took thee for a man!"

"I am no coward, my lord!" answered the student, in a deep, and half reproachful tone, "but I will not rashly throw away my life. The contents of that document are not for my eyes: to read it were scaling my own doom."

"Wherefore?"

"'Tis signed by the 'Ten,'" was the reply.

"By the 'Ten!'"

"As I do live, my lord, 'tis true."

"Well?"

"The usual warning, my lord, is given in the first part of it: 'Whoever dares to read this document, save he to whom it is directed, shall be visited by the vengance of the 'Ten.'"

"Ha! is it so?" exclaimed the stranger in a deep voice, "is it so? Then it is a sentence! No matter—I must know its contents. Look you, sir," he continued, "I'll give the choice of gold or instant death to resolve me the tenour of this parchment." Saying which, the stranger flung the letter and a purse upon the table, and drawing a dagger from beneath his cloak, he pointed the student to the table.

Calvari remained motionless.

"Wilt thou obey, or perish?" demanded the stranger, in a voice which made the chamber echo.

"Perish!" answered the student boldly.

The noble looked at him with apparent astonishment, then sheathing his dagger, he advanced towards the student, and in a voice in ill accordance with his words, exclaimed—"Fool! thou art only fit to mingle with the herd that so cravenly fear the 'Ten.' Thou hast a form and face that belie thy soul. I took thee for a man; one who had suffered, still suffers, and had heart enough to dare a struggle for his freedom. But I mistook thee—thou art a worm! The 'Ten' will rule thee, in sunlight and in darkness—at all times, in all places—thou art only fit to be a slave! Fear not me; I would not stain my blade with blood like thine. But, sir, a word with thee. If thou would'st henceforth revel in gold, go thou to-morrow to St. Mark's; seek the house of Count Foscari, and tell him, all potent as he is, there is another man in Venice,—one Count de Galliano,—who will overthrow him and the 'Ten.' Tell him this, and tell him too, that a plot is now afoot, to drive all tyrants from the soil of Venice, and that Count Galliano is at its head. Tell him, too, that we meet to-morrow night, in the vault of St. Mark's, and that our watchword is, 'The Orange Girl of Venice,'"

The student uttered a cry of recognition, and fell on his knees before the stranger.

CHAPTER II.

THE GONDOLIER.

On the day following the incidents in the preceding chapter, a nobleman approached a group of gondoliers, who were rattling dice on a little round table, in front of a low hostel, which stood in a long, broad street, leading from the grand square of St. Mark's, and fronting the sea. Small heaps of copper coin lay here and there upon the table; and it was evident, from the excited features of the players that the stakes, to them, were of an unusually large amount. One face of one of the party evinced but little symptoms of excitement, although, to the deep observing, there was more meaning, more real language, to be detected in his passionless features, than in those of his more frothy, and more talkative companions. His eyes were large, dark, lustrous and full; his forehead high, his hair thrown back, and falling in careless disorder adown his swarthy, sunburnt neck; his nose was Roman in its shape, with the nostrils wide and heavy, denoting the deep, fearless, and violent nature of their owner; his chin was bold, pointed, and covered with a heavy tuft of black and glossy hair; a heavy moustache covered his firm, upper lip, and his thick bull-like throat was exposed to the effects of the sun and atmosphere from the shoulders upward. He wore a loose, red shirt, with a broad, rumpled collar; the sleeves rolled up to the elbow, revealing a pair of stout, muscular, sunburnt arms, which seemed to bid defiance to the best stalwart compeer in the struggle for gondolier or wrestling fame. Yellow shoes, blue trowsers, fitting tightly to the skin, a rough, short, canvass frock, just reaching to the knees, and a leathern belt, with an enormous steel buckle in the front, completed the gondolier's attire. His height was slightly above the common, and his figure, as he half stood by, and half sat on, the edge of the rude table, displayed a suppleness and muscularity of limbs not often found among the everyday tenants of this habitable house, the world. The garb of his companions was similar to that of the bold gondolier, with the exception that, in general, his habiliments seemed tidier and cleanlier than theirs.

The master of the inn stood at the door, smoking his long, reed-like pipe, apparently with great satisfaction. Ever and anon, he cast his eyes furtively upon the gamesters, as if watching the progress of their games; and, at each result of the "last throw," a sickly, sarcastic smile would play around his mouth, revealing a set of teeth which seemed made to contrast in their whiteness with his dark and swarthy complexion. Judging him by his appearance, he could not have been far from five-and-forty years of age. He wore an apron of coarse, dirty muslin, and looked every inch the landlord of "the inn of St. Mary's." A stout, ill-favoured knave he seemed, and though while smoking, he paid, apparently, but little attention to the oaths and other exclamations of triumph or disappointment of those at the table, still a keen observer could easily have seen that not a word escaped his ear, nor a gesture of the gondoliers his eye.

As the noble approached. two or three of the gamesters threw down their dice, and, running towards him, proffered their services to row him out into the Lagoon, "if it was the noble signior's pleasure."

Passing them by unnoticed, the noble motioned the stout gondolier already described, to jump into his boat. The latter, with a respectful silence, sprang into his gondola, which lay moored beside a small flight of land stairs, directly in front of the hostel. The noble followed slowly, and took his seat in the stern, with a dignity which impressed the group on shore with an awe they could scarcely banish, even when the fleet bark had rounded the quay.

"Lie to," said the noble, when the boat had reached the centre of the Lagoon. "Dost thou know me?"

"I knew thee at the first," replied the gondolier, resting on his oars.

"How speeds the cause?" demanded the noble, in a low voice.

"Bravely, my lord; the innkeeper, Marco, hath a daring and patriotic heart. He hath gold, too, and will loan it to the cause, without interest."

"Good! and the rest?"

"They wear their dirks in their bosoms, 'twixt their flesh and shirts. Three hundred of them, as brave hearts as ever pulled oar or wielded knife, are ready to march at word of mine. When do we strike?"

"That will be determined to-night. I think 'twill be on carnival night; though I speak without authority. The number of men we can surely count on?"

"Three hundred."

"And all determined?"

"Every one, my lord."

"Speak lower, and title me not," said the noble, leaning forward in his seat. Since I have been travelling for assistance to our cause, I have learned that water and air have listening ears and tell-tale tongues, as well as dungeon or cavern walls. Why, man, the elements around us are witnesses to our speech; and strange things are told of how the ' Ten' have made even the waters, aye, and the floating atmosphere creatures of their will. Therefore, lest our voices betray us, speak thou in whispers : the lagoon, though broad and deep, hath, ere now, been the doom of many a votary of its bosom. Remember the fate of De Gama, and title me not. The ' Ten' are everywhere."

"Were it not better I should row about?" said the gondolier in a low tone. "If we should be watched from the shore by any of the spirits of the tribunal——"

"Right," replied the noble, "row on—but guide her farther from the shore."

"What success from abroad?" inquired the gondolier, slowly pulling outward.

"None," responded the other; "we must depend upon ourselves. Physical help is hopeless; although, in one shape, it is certain. I have raised twelve thousand ducats, in sound yellow coin, from certain citizens in Rome, Verona, and Cyprus, which now lies in a corner of the vault of St. Mark's : it will be shown tonight at our meeting."

"Gold may do much," observed the gondolier, meaningly.

"It will rouse the hearts of the desponding, if any be among us, when convened," said the noble, quickly; "for, to the vulgar mind, there is a power, yea, an eloquence, irresistible in a sack of shining dross. But, be that as it may, we have a doom even for the weak-hearted."

"Aye—the cord and knife!" observed the gondolier, with a slight curl of the lip. "Bah! 'tis too like the " Ten.'"

"Can they be dispensed with?" demanded the noble, quickly.

"They can," replied the gondolier, impetuously.

"How?" said the noble, earnestly.

"By depending on the honour of all who choose not to proceed," responded the gondolier.

"Pshaw! you know not men!" exclaimed the noble, hastily. "When men league themselves together for a mighty work, there must be a fear held out to bind them to be true. Else doubts and fears as to the success of the enterprise would be the forerunners only to desertions and betrayal. Men are not all true, all brave; and the weak nerve must be held in check, must be kept true, by the known brave, and the known true beside them; which latter failing, there must be a doom for apostates, which they must fear, to keep them true. For great ends, we must not scruple to employ small means. And what end, what enterprise more glorious than the freeing of one's country from a horde of villains that make all fear! They scruple not to shed our blood, they scruple not to tear away from life, on most trivial and uncertain causes, too, those they deem dangerous to themselves or to their power—and should we risk our lives, the lives of all united with us, by sparing one who knowing all our secrets, would depart on dastardly excuse, and peril the safety of us all? No; once colleagued, we must not risk life—perpetual freedom, and life's life—not for one, but all—high and low, the wealthy and the low born : and such an acme were endangered, to spare a craven's life, for sake of mercy!"

"I fear not betrayal," observed the gondolier, proudly.

"Nor I," replied the noble, " while we have a doom for traitors. But, enough of this. I called last night on our spy in the eastern section. Wouldst believe it —he knew me not."

"Ha! not know thee!" exclaimed the gondolier, leaning forward on his oars. "Has he turned traitor?"

"In good faith! not he," replied the noble. "It was my beard and face, and dress he knew not."

"By St. Mark! I feared something else!" said the gondolier, half smiling "What number reports he ready for trial hour?"

"Four hundred and twelve," answered the noble. "Their names are registered on parchment. In truth, that same student is a brave worker; his parchments contain the names of every member of our order, in characters as plain and bold as ever came from the hand of man. Our constitution and our laws, our rewards and penalties—the progress of our order and its history—the causes of our existence—the wrongs we have suffered, the injuries forborne—in fine, our order's whole history—are traced in characters of truth upon his parchments. His daily journal keeps he; of the proselytes made, wrongs suffered, the day and hour of the deed, and the names of the wronged and the wrongers. A terrible history of life lies in those parchments; a terrible history of blood, lust, murder, and oppression, which cries aloud to Heaven for vengeance."

"And it will come, ere long!" exclaimed the gondolier, with a savage smile.

"Aye, it will," cried the noble, in a deep tone, though without stirring a hair,—"it will—aye, it shall!—and when it does, woe, woe to the doers of dark deeds! woe to the tribunal! woe to the 'Ten!'"

"Amen! with all my heart!" exclaimed the gondolier, slowly pulling his oars.

"Now, to what I would tell thee," added the noble, leaning forward a little, and resting his elbow on the rim of the boat. "The old Count of Romagna has been missing these three days; and his motherless daughter, the Lady Isabel, is all but mad in consequence. The count's friends speak of his absence with a pallid cheek and a faltering tongue. 'Tis evident that they suspect, and yet—the cravens!—they dare not give utterance, with their tongues, to that which is seen so plainly in their eyes!"

"Hast thou no suspicion of his fate?" said the gondolier, earnestly.

"I have," replied the noble, drawing a small roll of parchment from his belt. 'The Lady Isabel herself did, but yesterday, put into my hands this note, traced in characters recognisable only by those familiar with the handwriting of the president of the infernal tribune. Listen: it runneth thus,—

"This day, Friday, the 9th, 4 of the dial.

"Thomaso Romagna, we summon thee to appear before us within the hour.
          (Signed)   "THE TEN."

The gondolier turned pale.

"Thou seest the necessity of action," said the noble, on perceiving the change in the countenance of his companion. "Thou seest the manner in which we live; we, the rightful inheritors of our beloved Venice—we, the strong-armed and lion-hearted—we, the descendants of the fathers of the Adriatic's chosen isle—we, the favoured and the gifted of nature and of God! Shall we endure it—shall we suffer these upstarts of power to trample upon the God-chartered rights of Venetians, and crush us at their will? Shall we live on, in base and abject fear—shall we crawl, like worms, before these soulless heart-spotted lepers, till either nature, accident, or tyranny, tears us from such mind and body vassalage? Shall we endure to have the bravest and purest blood amongst us rifled from our midst, and not raise a hand to smite the murderers? Forbid it, God of my fathers! while there yet exists a son of Venice wise enough to detect, and brave enough to strike at, villany and her myrmidons!"

The gondolier pulled his oars lustily, fearing that the excited gestures, and bold, loud voice of his companion would be observed by those on shore.

"Think'st thou he is dead?" asked the gondolier, striving to turn the excitement of the noble back to its former cautious current.

"Think he is dead!" exclaimed the count, in a lower tone. "If I thought so, if I thought there existed the slightest shadow of a hope that the old man was yet alive, all Venice should ring with the war-cry of Galliano! Think he is dead! the summons of the victim of the 'Ten' is but another word for—'Thou art marked and doomed—come to thy death!'"

"But the cause?" inquired the gondolier, pale with terror at the loud voice of his companion, and rowing rapidly farther out from the shore.

"Foscari's son!" was the reply; "Foscari's son,—that insolent, purse-proud dastard,—proposed to the Lady Isabel to become his mistress !—Dost hear it, his mistress—she, the daughter of a race of nobles, old as Venice itself, and whose scutcheon had never known stain! His mistress! his! aye, the mistress of a mongrel heart, that never had courage enough to strike a whining dog! His mistress! Ha! ha! ha! Oh, that I had been by, to have smote him for the word! He proposed, I say, in dastard speech, to Lady Isabel, and was ejected from the lord's house he had insulted. Stung with rage and mortification, he forged a lie, and told it to his father. In an hour, the black messenger of the tribunal summoned him before the "Ten." He bowed, and seizing his hat and cloak, left the house, in company with the note bearer, without even taking leave of, or bidding adieu to, his daughter. While leaving the room, he dropped the summons, which the Lady Isabel picked up. She tried to read it, but the warning sentence was the first that met her eye, and though she kept, she did not dare to read it. But yesterday, she gave it to me—but yesterday, I saw her, like a lily which once had reared its head in towering pride, now bowed to the earth with the shafts of sorrow and despair! She sits now, in her home, a motherless, fatherless girl; with no friend nor brother to save her from the importunities and insults of the dastard, who robbed her of her father!"

The cheek of the gondolier crimsoned a moment, with rage and scorn; when the blood fell back into its channels again, leaving his features pale as marble.—Dark and terrible were his thoughts; and, though he grasped his oar, till the nails almost entered the wood, he spoke not. The noble felt conscious that he had touched a string in the breast of his companion, which would not soon die away; and, pointing silently to the shore, the gondola was soon back to the spot from which it started.

As many were lounging about the door of the hotel, the noble sprung hastily from the boat, saying, in a low voice, as he passed the gondolier,—

"Remember to-night! The vault of St. Mark's!"

CHAPTER III.

THE PRIDE OF VENICE.

IT was a night of beauty and of music, in Venice. The vault of heaven seemed like an eternal canopy of darkest velvet, thickly gemmed with silver, and crowned with a ball of fire. The housetops, the balconies, the vestibules, the gardens, streets, and quays, were thronged with the young and old, of both sexes, drinking the evening ether. The moon-kissed waters were covered with fantastically arrayed gondolas, from which arose the ripe, rich voices of the gay young roysterers and cavaliers in melodious song: while from others the flute and guitar mingled their music with the floating zephyrs, rendering the whole a fairy scene. It was a night of harvest to those who loved the bright and beautiful; it was a night of harvest to the maidens whose lovers had been coyish in naming the hour for betrothal before high Heaven; it was a night of harvest to the aged and infirm, for their pains and rheums were dissipated by the mellowness and liveliness of the air; it was the harvest night of gondoliers, and musicians, and drink venders; and it was the harvest night of the sorrowing ones; the beauties of earth, air, and sky—the veriest beauties—made their sorrow lighter, their griefs less poignant, their woes less dark, less terrible; it was a night when the grief-stricken could smile without deeming it a sacrilege; it was a night when foes thought kindlier of each other, and were half disposed to forget injuries past, and to look kindly on ▩▩▩ of the future. Who has not seen such nights in the course of life's ▩▩▩

has ever seen them in such perfection as they were found in Venice in the merry
month of June?

On the night described, two young females, evidently of high rank, were walking
up and down the gravelled walks of a private and beautifully-finished garden,
adorned with statues and a small fountain. They were dressed in darkest mourning,
and without ornament of any kind. Their hands were linked together as they
walked, and their voices were low as doves, when whispering the feelings of their
hearts. A wall of some ten feet guarded them from the intrusion and observation
of those without; when an old, white-headed servant, who sat on a cushioned
bench on the porch of the house, attested at once the fearfulness and chariness of
character of the females. The appearance of the elder—for there was evidently a
discrepancy in their years—was that of a maiden of about twenty summers. She
was slightly above the common height of her sex, and had a full, high and beautifully polished forehead; her nose was Grecian, and the mould of her lips like unto
a perfect bow; her chin was slightly pointed, yet dimpled; her eyes large, and black
as night; her hair, of which there was a profusion, was black and silky, and was
parted tastefully in the centre of her brow, and hung in wavy masses adown her
snowy neck. A narrow collar of the whitest lace, hemmed the neck of her dark
velvet frock, and gave to her figure a beauty which could scarcely be idealised by
a painter. Her dress fitted tightly to her waist and arms, and her hands were
hid by gloves of white kid. The costume of her companion was precisely the same;
but though the features and figure of the latter were smaller, less imposing, less
striking, less beautiful, still they had in them something more winning something
more pleasing, something more congenial to the humble soul. Her brow was of a
moderate height, and its complexion was like that of one accustomed to wander
in the sunlight, fearless of the effects of such exposure upon the skin; her lips
were small, her eyes moderately large, but full of lustre, full of love, full of
gentleness, confidence, and kindness. Her chin was bold, but it was a softened
boldness; her neck was beautifully shaped and full, but it was of the shape that
artists love to draw from, not the neck which creates passion in the sensualist.
Her form was perfect in its proportions; but it was one of those forms which
strike the eye of the gentle heart, not the proud, the brave, the impassioned. It
was a short, delicate form; and one which seemed to tell the looker-on, that it
was a spirit-sojourner here, not a human one; that it was a tender plant formed
bloom in the most carefully cultivated and most tenderly watched plats, not in
the rough, wind-exposed spots, of God's green garden—earth.

They were, evidently, not sisters in kin, but it was also evident that they were
more than sisters in love. Perhaps suffering had made them such; perhaps, trial;
but whatever the cause, though strangers in blood, they were, without question,
sisters in heart.

The old servant who sat on the porch kept his eyes upon them with a look of
love and affection, which attested his anxiety for their welfare. And when any-
thing like a smile played around the lips of either, his own heart bounded and his
own cheeks were enlivened more cheerily than theirs. It was something worth
looking after, we opine, or the old man would not have watched so earnestly for
a smile from either of the females.

Whatever the subject of their discourse, it was dissipated by a servant, who
entered from the house, stating that a gentleman would see the Lady Isabella.

"His name?" demanded the elder of the ladies.

"He'll not reveal it, my lady," answered the servant.

"His age?" inquired the lady.

"He is turned of sixty, lady," replied the servant.

"Say I will wait on him," responded the lady, majestically.

The servant bowed and withdrew.

"Shall I remain here?" inquired the younger lady.

"Yes Eugenia," replied Isabel, with emotion, "talk to aged Philippo, on the
porch yonder though not an Adonis, he is yet a merry talker; and, in good

truth, he can while an hour away as pleasantly as many a younger of this make."

Though the Lady Isabel spoke with an attempt at pleasantry, there was yet a sadness in her tone which touched the heart of her companion, and brought a tear into her eye.

They kissed each other, and the elder slowly entered the house.

When the Lady Isabella entered the reception room, an old man, sitting on a high cushion near the window, and dressed in a gay and flashy suit illy becoming his years, met her eye. A crafty and sinister expression played around his small thin lips, and sharp, ferret-like eyes. He wore a pointed beard, and mustachios, white as the driven snow, and both, to all appearance, cultivated with the extremest care. His eye-brows were white and sloping, which gave to his visual organs the appearance of having been set in without regard to taste, propriety,

No. 2.

or fashion. His forehead was low, but the absence of hair upon the crown made it, at first view, appear lofty. He was dressed in a scarlet jacket and shoulder cloak, and trunks and hose of the finest and whitest silk. He wore slippers with white rosettes, and a long, slender rapier was slung around his waist, upon the hilt of which both his hands rested, as Isabel entered the apartment.

"Your pleasure, sir?" demanded the lady, sitting on a raised cushion, opposite him.

"I have called on an errand, lady," said the stranger, "which involves thy safety, and the lives of all thy kin. I would first ask if thou art aware of the existence of a young noble called Galliano?"

"I am," replied the lady, slightly blushing.

"I would further ask, lady," continued the old man, "if thou hast seen him within three days?"

"Why these questions?" said the lady, turning slightly pale.

"'Tis thine office to answer, not to question, lady," replied the old man, with a sarcastic smile, and rivetting his bold and crafty eyes upon the lady.

"What if I answer not?" inquired Isabel, proudly.

"Means will be found to make thee answer, lady," responded the old man, smiling, and in a tone which made the young lady's heart sink with terror. "There are means for the performance of everything, lady," he continued in the same biting, sneering tone, "and it will argue wisdom in thee not to provoke the engines of wrath. Thy father did, and thou now wearest sables for his imprudence."

The cheek of Isabel now turned ghastly white; her bosom panted with emotion, and a tear leapt into her eye; but, after a silent but violent struggle, she forced it back, and, rising, approached the table, as if to ring a little bell, which stood upon it. The stranger, divining her intent, suddenly rose, caught her by the wrist, and exclaimed, in a low but biting tone,—

"Lady, be not in haste to call your servants,—I can leave your house without their aid. Besides this is not a question of politeness, but one of life and death. So, oblige me taking my blunt speech as it suits you, till I am done. Pray, be seated!" And he led her, with scrupulous politeness back to her seat.

"The gallants of our sea-girt isle, call thee the Pride of Venice," continued the old man, seating himself opposite Isabel, and gazing at her with a cold and brazen eye. "See what it is to be beautiful, lady,—see what it is to have an angel's stamp on human lineaments! Reflect what it is to have youth and hot blood and all the appetites for the luxuries and pleasures, invented by man to charm youth and the summer of life! And ponder over the beauties and luxuries, generously accorded to all human kind by Nature, to make man, from his first to his second childhood, feel the enjoyments created for his sole benefit. Connect them with the luxuries conceived and perfected by man, and then feel the poignancy of the thought that human hands have doomed thee to taste no more of either—have doomed thee to the eternal sleep found only in the grave!"

Isabel spoke not; though her cheeks blanched every moment paler, her eyes quailed not at the steady and brazen gaze of the man now before her, but her heart throbbed painfully rapid.

"What if thou wert doomed, lady?" continued the old man, in a tone indicating, in spite of himself, his disappointment in not receiving any response to his observations.

"I—" said Isabel, faintly, as a sickly pallor darted across her features.

"Ay, lady," added the old man, "what if thou wert doomed?"

"I'd meet it, like my father," replied Isabel, firmly.

"So thou say'st now," said the old man, with a quiet and cold smile; "but, if thou stood'st in a chamber whose walls were bare as thine own limbs of vesture, with the engines of death girding thee around, while the grim forms of scurvily clad and masked executioners stood waiting the signal of their master to rend thy bones asunder,—thy speech would falter as thy cheek now doth blanch!"

"What is thy errand here?" demanded Isabel, in a low, deep voice.

" To warn thee beware a traitor," answered the old man, " to warn thee cease all communication with one to whom thou givest too free licence with thine ear and lip. For shame on thee ! that one so highly born—an orphan, too !—should think so lightly of her honour as to permit the free addresses of a known libertine and—"

" Stop thy dastard tongue!" exclaimed the Lady Isabel, starting up, and pointing the old man to the door,—" whoe'er thou art—whate'er thine errand—I care not ! Begone."

" Lady,———"

" Not a word ! This house—this roof is mine—mine, by heritage and law—mine, by the legal codes of Venice—and, while beneath my own roof, no low-born hind, nor creature of birth or power, shall assail mine ear with insolence, or bravado. Begone !"

The old man leaned upon his cane, between her and the door, his feathered cap hanging in his left hand, and his eyes gloaming maliciously and sharply at the fair speaker as she stood, stern, bold and erect, her finger pointing to the door.

" Lady, I am here for a purpose," said he, in a low, soft voice, and with a smile which was an index to his nature, " I am here for a purpose, and till it be accomplished, thy threshold shall calmly await my inclination to cross it."

" What ho, Martino !" exclaimed Isabel, loudly, and ringing a silver bell which rested on the circular table, " what ho, Martino ! thy mistress needs thy help !"

The object of her wrath, smiling, quietly resumed his seat.

A hurried step was heard in the entry—the door opened hastily, and a young servitor, of seven and twenty years, entered the apartment.

" The matter, lady !" he exclaimed, hurriedly and bowing.

" Turn yon hoary wretch from out of my doors !" she cried, pointing to her visitor.

The eyes of the servitor and the old man met—a hasty sign from the latter, un-observed by the Lady Isabel, but which the sharp eye of the servitor detected, silenced the latter and caused his cheek to blanch to the hue of ashes.

" Leaves us," said the old man, in a calm and silvery tone.

Without a word—without an upraised look—without a glance at his astonished mistress, the servitor bowed, and, his eyes resting upon the carpet, slowly retired from the apartment.

Isabel looked after him in astonishment.

" Thou seest the engines of thy house," observed the old man, sardonically, " thou seest the faith of its small pillars !"

The Lady Isabel heeded him not, but clasped her hand to her forehead, staggered, pale and ghastly, to a cushion, and sank upon it speechless.

———

CHAPTER IV.

THE sun was playing through the casement when the Lady Isabel awoke, and the hum of voices mingled with the winds. She looked round. The door was closed ; and save herself, no human thing breathed in the chamber. The apartment seemed smaller than usual, and the drapery around the walls seemed darker than on the preceding day. A large and heavy lock was on the door too ; and the door itself had changed its colour since yesternight. The entire aspect of the apartment seemed changed. A picture—a small one—hung between the windows which she could not recollect. She sprang up, and advanced towards it—she did not know it. Her brow felt heated—her eyes weak and nervous. She sat down on a cushion, and tried to think—she could not. A short pain shot athwart her brow, and scattered the loose leaves of her memory. She felt sick at heart, chilled n soul, vacant in mind. A phantom seemed to dance before her—a dim and shadowy phantom—yet could she not give it shape; for when her eyes gazed intently and boldly at it, it vanished, and the sunbeams were before her. She arose, and paced the chamber vacantly. Something heavy was on her heart—an iron weight upon her brow. Air! air! Her tongue was parched—her lips seemed glued together.

" Water—water !" she muttered, unconsciously.

She paused—her eyes rivetted upon a narrow slit in the carpeted floor. It gradually widened, till a square hole, of some four feet, revealed a dark vault beneath. She stood fixed, gazing into the depth, which appeared like the chasm of eternity. Presently, a slender and curiously carved wash-stand, with a snowy towel dangling at its side, rose, as if by some springy pressure, and, when its base had reached the carpet's edge, the wooden floor resumed its place, and the stand, surmounted by a circular basin of brass, filled with scented water, remained motionless. She gazed upon it half vacantly, a moment; then plunged her hand into the liquid and applied it to her brow. Memory seemed to return shadowingly with the first drop of the cooling liquid, and frantically seizing the towel and bathing it in the bowl, she applied it to her burning brow. A sob, a cry, burst from her parched lips, and she sank overpowered upon the floor. As if by magic, the stand immediately disappeared—the casements darkened, and a huge torch rose through an opening in the floor. The drapery on the wall opposite the windows was thrown aside, and a young and magnificently dressed cavalier entered and raised the inanimate lady in his arms. A smile hovered around his lips, as he gazed upon the fevered 'lip and ashy cheek of his burden. A smile—but it was not the smile of love nor guilt. Raising her in his strong arms, he silently and stealthily departed with his burthen, through the secret panel, behind the drapery.

The torch still burned on.

CHAPTER V.

THE KINSMAN'S TALE.

It was eventide; the stars shone dimly in the heavens, and the moon was pale The atmosphere after a warm and sultry day, was cool and pleasant, and infused new strength into the feeble, and made the couch of the despairing invalid a couch of hope. It was one of those nights when the nervous mind feels settled, joyous, strong, and fearless; one of those nights when the timorous heart is sanguine of success, and fears not to make a venture; one of those nights when the malig- nant heart is so acted upon by the elements, that its dark conceptions centre on one spot, and that a bloody one—when it is in such a state that one kind word from its hated foe would change its venom into love; one of those nights when the woe- stricken and the trampled of God's make half forget their wrongs, their injuries, their sorrows, calamities, and woes, and feel cheerful, half joyous, more than re- signed; one of those nights, when, if ever, angels in heaven look down upon mortality with a hope and a smile; one of those nights when earth has more laugh- ing, joyous ones, and less weeping and groaning ones—one of those nights when the King of the eternities says to the recording angel, " Cease thy recording labours—crime sleeps."

Venetians of every grade promenaded the streets, squares, and quays. The tide was high, and almost on a level with the piers. The lagoons were covered with the richly caparisoned barges and gondolas of the nobility and higher classes of citizens; while the humble gondolier, his bark freighted with young lovers, pulled his oars cheerily, as the ripe, rich voices of his passengers chaunted their favourite melodies. It was a night of univsrsal joy. Universal? No, there were exceptions. Despite the cool and delicious air—despite the joy which seemed so universal, there were two that night in Venice upon whose cheeks no joy, no smile, nor aught betokening mirth or happiness, could be detected. An old man, with locks snowy as the vesture of the highest Alps in winter, and clad in coarse, brown velvet trunks, and a jacket of the same, sat on the edge of the Orfano canal, bathing his feet in the tide. Beside him, half-extended, his elbow resting on the earth, and his head supported by his broad, sinewy hand, was a young, stout, well-proportioned youth, of some four-and-twenty years, clad in the garb of a gondolier.

"What a beautiful night, Paulo!" exclaimed the elder, glancing at his companion; "it half tempts one to forget his griefs, and think Venice a free land! 'Tis a shame, boy, that thy barge was broken at the regatta on Monday last. It would have been money in thy pouch, to-night—for, look! all Venice hath disgorged its living, and they float upon the lagoons like water-fish. The young maid leans upon her lover's arm, and, happy now, dreams that the future hath in it no more of joylessness. Umph! she'll find her mistake out, ere the world hath done with her. Boy," he added, "dost recollect thy sister?"

" Ay, father," replied the other, sadly.

"Dost recollect her beauty, boy, her angelic smile, her heavenly eyes, her spirit-like form, her tiny feet, and lady-like hands, so small, so white? We used to call her our 'little belle.' Throughout Venice she was called 'the pretty orange girl.' She used to sell her fruit on sunny days, in her little round basket, ornamented with orange leaves. Everybody used to buy of her, she was so fair, and had such winning ways with her! Dost remember her perfectly, boy?"

" Ay, father ay," replied the youth, in a deep guttural voice.

"And then her voice, too—so ripe, so rich, so mellow, that, when she pleased she could lull the sternest heart into the calmest, gentlest humour, and make it sad, or joyous, as she willed, Ah! she was too fair, too beautiful for earth!"

A tear danced a moment on the lid of the old man's eye, then leaped upon his rough and hoary cheek. He brushed it off—a moment afterwards, and the snowy locks that covered his crown were not more pale than his tear-kissed cheek.

" 'Tis now three years since she was taken from us," continued the old man, as if speaking to himself, "and yet no word, no trace of her? Boy," he added sternly, "had'st thou but the spirit, the fire, the bold blood that should mark thine age, thy father's spirit would, in the winter of its years, take its last look of Venice and of earth, with a smile!"

" What mean'st thou, father?" cried the youth, starting up, with surprise.

" What do I mean—what do I mean?" muttered the old man sarcastically, "ay boy, what do I mean?"

" Speak out father," cried Paulo, earnestly.

" Foscari!" said the old man, laconically.

" Well?"

" He robbed thy sister of her honour, and yet lives."

" Remember his birth, father!"

" His birth?"

" Ay, father, his birth—remember that."

" Too well, too well do I remember it," muttered the old man, satirically. " Too well do I remember it; my heart is like a burning coal when I remember it."

" What would'st have me do, father?"

" Avenge her wrongs—hadst thou the heart!"

" Have I it not, father?"

" Thy conduct doth not show it, boy."

" The hour hath not yet come, father."

" Dost look for it, Paulo?"

" I watch for it, father."

" Watch for it! The brave heart and cunning mind make time, and for revenge wait not for circumstance or accident. I'll tell thee a tale, boy. When I was thine age, or near it, I loved thy mother. We were poor, both; we were young both; we were comely, both. She had no superior in beauty among the haughties or lowliest, in Venice, of her sex. For her beauty's sake a young lord wooed her —wooed her, but wooed her not to wed her. He dazzled her eyes with his gold, rank, and promises. She was weak enough to believe that she would disgrace his birth, pride, and rank, by wedding a lowly craftsman's daughter ; and therefore, though professing much before to love me, discarded me. Knowing well the motives of the noble's visits to her cottage, I confronted him one night upon the Rialto, as he was returning from her house, and charged him with his vile intents. He answered me with a look only—a look of supercilious scorn—and bade me stand out of his path. Persons were passing at the moment. and I obeyed him meekly. He passed on, with a loud, scornful laugh. My blood was up—but the hour had not yet come. The moon was up, the stars were forth, in all their light and beauty—it was not the hour! Fearful of death, he did not venture to cross the Rialto again by night, for a week, when, conquering his timidity, he donned his plume and sword, and cloak, and posted for her house. She had been expecting him, and was arrayed in her most glittering and showy attire. She looked beautiful, and knew it. She stood at the door anxiously awaiting his arrival. The night was dark, and the streets and quays were dimly lighted. Concealed behind the gate of an adjoining house, I heard every whisper that passed between them. She had promised to become his on the ensuing night. It was to be a secret marriage—to be kept concealed at first—then gradually broached to his family and hers.

"Thou understandest the meaning of such a marriage, Paulo. I heard it all—understood it all. My heart was rent with jealousy and rage, and yet I kept my post, till he quitted her to return home. Taking off my shoes, so that my foot-falls should not alarm his ear, I stealthily followed him, till he had arrived within ten paces of the Rialto. Then drawing my knife, I rushed upon him, and the blade had thrice entered his heart ere he could recover from his surprise. A groan—the faint groan of the despairing, escaped his lips, and he lay upon the pavement, lifeless as a stone. No human ear. save mine, had heard his fall—no human eye, save mine, had seen the deed. I rolled him in his cloak, and dragged him to the lagoon hard by. A pile of stones lay near, from which I gathered a dozen of the largest, and placed them on the body ; then taking a cord from my girdle, carefully tied the cloak around them all, and plunged the bulk into the watery tide. It sank, and, till now, no human ear hath heard of the fate of our doge's elder brother."

"'Twas a base and bloody deed !" exclaimed the gondolier, shuddering, as he turned his gaze away from the old man, and looked fearfully around to see if other ears beside his own had listened to the dark recital.

"A base and bloody deed !" repeated the other, mockingly ; " a base and bloody deed ! Pah ! He would have slain thy mother's honour, robbed me of peace for life, and made wanton with a score of hearts as fond, as trusting as hers—perchance driven a hundred others into despair, like me—had I not slain him. Pah ! He was a villain, and deserved it. He was a noble, and the trampler on peace, virtue, and honesty ; he had well nigh murdered my peace for ever, and for that act, I became mine own avenger. But mark, how his kindred have avenged him—his nephew, the present young Foscari, beguiled, seduced my only daughter —thy sister—and yet he is at large—branded eternal shame upon her erst innocent forehead, and upon mine and thine, and yet he lives to play the same pranks upon others. Thou knowest that that vile deed of his sent the heart and hairs of thy mother with anguish to the tomb, and made a wanton of thy sister, and made the ruin of our house what it is, and all but broke the heart of him who wooed her ere Foscari laid his serpent eyes upon her to lure her on to ruin—and yet he lives, and so do I—I, in weakness and grey hairs ; and so dost thou—thou, in young manhood's vaunted strength and fire ! 'The hour hath not come,' thou say'st. Three years have flown since first the dastardly deed was consummated, and yet for thee and vengeance, 'the hour hath not yet come !' Out upon thee, coward, boy !"

"Father, father," groaned the young gondolier, passionately, "crush not my spirit by branding me with such opprobrious names. Coward! boy! Oh!"

"What art thou else?" said the old man, gibingly, and glancing maliciously at his son. "What art thou else? Where is the bold spirit, where the lion-daring that should mark thy years? For three years hath the cloud of wrong floated over our house—for three long years hath the finger of scorn pointed at us as varlets that patiently submit to infamy, oppression, indignity, without the courage to raise a finger to smite the villain down. Three long years of shame, opprobrium, three long years—an old man, I—a young man, thou! Three long years of unavenged shame—three long years—think of that!"

The young gondolier groaned deeply. He buried his head in his broad, tanned hands, and wept like a child.

"Has thou a soul—a heart, a brain, an eye, a hand?" persisted the old man, hissingly. "Hast either of these—and yet wearest shame, cowardice, upon thy brow? Hast thou a heart, a hand, I say, and dost thou play the woman's game, —watching. Out on thee, craven!"

"Father!"

"Not a word!—not a word! and dare not call me by that name again, or I shall smite thee. 'Father!' Who gave thee the right to call me by that name? Dost dare to call thyself of my blood—my name—my race? 'Father!' Now, as I live! I do believe thee to be the spawn of some chicken-hearted dastard whose wily arts exchanged thee, in infancy, for mine own proud souled and fearless child, when my wife was absent. Go to! thou art no son of mine!"

The chafed spirit of the young gondolier could stand no more. He sprang upon the old man, and, grasping him by the collar, with one stern and sudden jerk, stretched him, lengthwise, upon the pavement; then planting one knee upon his breast, he, with his disengaged hand, drew a long, narrow blade from his girdle and, raising it aloft, exclaimed,—

"If thou wouldst have me an assassin, what subject so fit to dye this yet unstained knife, as thine own foul carcase? Another word—another taunt—and though thou wert ten times my father, thou'lt find I am not the poor, patient, gibe-bearing spaniel thou deemest me."

"Let go thy hold!" cried the old man, struggling and writhing, as the white foam of passion gathered around his lips. Let go thy hold, or I shall call for help!"

"Call on, I care not!" exclaimed the gondolier, huskily, "call on, I care not, even if thou shouldst be answered by the all potent 'Ten'!"

"The Ten!" said a low, deep voice beside him. "The Ten! it is a terrible power to defy!"

The gondolier started at the unexpected and thrilling voice. Did he know it? Was there a magic spell in its deep rich tone, that his ear recognised an old acquaintance? His fingers let go their clutch of the prostrate fruit-vendor—the knife dropped from his hand—his face lost its passionate flush, and was usurped by a chalk-like paleness. He rose from his threatening position by the old man, and catching the eye and cloaked form of the stranger, dropped upon one knee before him, saying,—

"What wouldst thou, master?"

"Does such an attitude become a Venetian?" said the stranger impatiently; "To thy feet, man—to thy feet!"

The gondolier, crimsoning to the temples, started up, and suddenly doffing his plumeless cap, with downcast eyes, and in a voice husky with shame and emotion, inquired,—

"Art in need?"

"I am," replied the stranger, softly; "a burden not far from hence needs thy carrying. I have had a heavy task of it, myself, this hour, and need aid. Canst go?"

"I can."

"Then follow me."

They left the spot together ; and, ere the old fruit-vendor could recover from the effects of their sudden meeting and departure, the stranger and gondolier were out of sight.

"There's more in this than I can fathom," said the old man, pondering over the strange scene ; "there is matter touching the state in't ! Who is yon stranger? Methinks I've seen his face before, but where—where? I cannot recal the time or place. Some high-born scion, doubtless—common blood hath no such eyes, no such face, no such voice, no such step, no such trappings, as his ! What can it mean ? Paulo trembled, lost manhood, fire, dignity, passion at his voice ! Some dark game's a-foot ! The state needs cleaning—I've heard Paulo mutter in his sleep. If he be engaged in a conspiracy to sweep off all our lordly tyrants—if he be !"—a strange light, like the enthusiastic gleam sometimes seen in the eyes of youth, shone in the fruit-vendor's dark orbs—"if he be ! why, then, his father's benison go with him ! Oh, that I were young again—young as my brave, wronged boy—with what a heart I'd plunge into the midst of these conspirators, and be one of them. I would—I would—I would ! But I am old—weak—half-falling into my grave. No, no; I must think of other things than blood. The state must be cleaned by the young—the down-trodden avenged by the young. Old men can but preach. And yet, how I have wronged poor Paulo ! how wrongly charged him. ' He watches for the hour !' I see it all, now—I see it all ! How I have wronged him !—my poor, wronged daughter will yet be avenged."

With thoughts and mutterings like these, the fruit-vendor hied him homeward.

CHAPTER VI.

THE COMPANION.

THEY walked on, the stranger and the gondolier. They kept side by side, and spoke in low tones. They walked on firmly, yet nervously, as if on each step the existence of an empire depended. The streets, and squares, and quays were now alive with the young and aged, of every class, returning to their homes. The deep-toned bell of St. Mark's fell upon their ears, and throughout Venice its heavy toll warned the populace that it lacked but an hour of midnight. The moon and stars waxed paler and dimmer every moment, till the stranger and his companion could scarce see their way. Still they walked on. Wished they for darkness?

The moon and stars were hid. The whole vault of heaven was curtained with drapery, dark and thick and frightful. It seemed as if man's last hope had been cut off—as if Deity had drawn a sheet of darkness between his throne and earth, that his already offended eye might be no more offended by the deeds of darkness committed by man upon his fellow man. Yet the elements were not at peace :—the winds played bo-peep with each other on the Lagoons and throughout the corners of old Venice, as if to frighten the few still awake, and to arouse to wakeful fear the thousands sleeping.

They wandered on, the gondolier and the stranger. They had already traversed half of Venice, and yet had not reached their goal, if goal they had in view.

They had neared the Rialto, still in conversation earnest as when they had first set out, when the watchful eye of the stranger discerned lights ahead. He laid his hand upon the arm of his companion, and pointing to the advancing torches, both noiselessly and cautiously drew back, and concealed themselves behind a broad, towering pillar at the base of the bridge.

"Now," whispered the stranger to his companion, "now, thou wilt see the scourge of our fair isle ; now, thou wilt behold the instruments of that power, the very name of which makes the cheek of childhood turn pale, and the nerves of gay youth and stern manhood turn watery. Behold, but speak not—stir not—breathe not ; nay, utter not a word, though the victim be thine own sire !"

"I will not," said his companion.

"Hush—they come !"

In silence, and with slow and solemn step, a double file of guards, six on each side, and each bearing a naked, double-edged sword, crossed the Rialto, and passed the pillar behind which the stranger and his companion were concealed. In their midst, with ponderous and muffled chains around his wrists, was a young man of some seven-and-twenty years, in the garb of a gondolier. A tall, half-naked,

No. 3.

swarthy-complexioned slave, bearing a torch in one hand, guarded either side of the prisoner ; while before and behind the little troop marched one in the costume of a cowled monk, with a long, white cross in his right hand, carried carelessly like a cane.

"Ha!" exclaimed the gondolier, as his eye fell upon the prisoner's face, " 'tis——"

But ere he could complete the sentence, the hand of the stranger was upon his mouth.

The procession with its victim passed on, and, turning an angle of the square, was soon lost to view.

" Rash man!" exclaimed the stranger, reproachfully, "would'st betray us ?"

But the latter answered not—a film was before his eyes—his whole frame shook with terror and emotion — and he sank into the arms of the stranger, speechless.

The winds whistled, and the Rialto seemed almost on the point of giving way before the violence of the gale.

CHAPTER VII.

THE STORM.

THE belfry of St. Mark's gave a solitary toll ; the gale swept around the old tower, and gave to its chime a heavy, stern, iron-like sound, which seemed almost powerful enough to re-awake to time and being the tomb-sleepers of old Venice. The wail of the increasing gale seemed like a dirge of devils over the corse of their king, in the royal chamber of the Shades. The Rialto shook as if an earthquake were coursing beneath its foundations.

The gale was at its height. As if the ministers of Deity had been ordered to level their several shafts at earth and destroy it, the windows of heaven were opened—of lightning, flash succeeded flash, and peal followed peal of thunder— the rain came rushing down upon the seemingly-doomed city—and the angry blast flew around the squares and lagoons as if determined to make a chaos of the isle towering above the waters. Mothers, with their infants in their arms, started out of their beds affrighted, and with their nurslings, crouched in corners and dark places to hide them from the broad, bright flashes of the red lightning, and the deafening roars of the booming thunder. Young and tender-hearted brides crept, shudderingly, from their couches, and dropped upon their knees, in prayer. Old men, hoary with age and crime, turned pale, and mumbled half-broken sentences of long-forgotten prayers. Widowed matrons, upon their knees, sent up supplications to the throne of the Most High, for sons exposed to the dangers of the angry deep; and youthful and hoary monks counted their beads and said earnest prayers that He would yet spare the criminal city for repentance.

The waters of the lagoons were swollen to a fearful height, deluging the piers and streets, and sweeping off into the tide of the broad Adriatic every floating thing that came within their reach. Yet all was darkness, save when, ever and anon, the gleam of some fitful flash exposed the havoc of the storm.

The stranger, cloaked, bent over the senseless gondolier, who lay in a sitting posture, at the base of the pillar, and shielded him from the descending rain ; though drenched to the skin, the noble cared not for himself, but had every thought centered upon the peril of his companion.

" Terror hath unnerved, unwitted him," he muttered, " and the discord and battle of the elements have not in them enough of power to wake him !"

The tide rose higher, and the noble felt the water entering his shoes. Quick as thought, he raised the inanimate gondolier from his perilous position, and dragged him up the bridge. This sudden movement, together with the sharp, heavy and rapid beatings of the rain, roused the latter from his stupor. He started, and put out his hands wildly—for the darkness prevented his eyes from being of any service—and he felt the cloak and hand of the noble. At this moment, a brigh flash revealed the face of the latter, and the evening's events rushing through his mind, he cried out :—

"Still here? Let us fly!"

"Whither?" responded the noble, as a chill ran through his frame at sight of the ghastly features of his companion. "Whither? The streets and piers and squares are deluged, and the Rialto alone affords refuge from the waters. Here we must abide till the storm gives o'er!"

"But we shall die here!"

"Die! Fear it not: fate hath not yet spoken such decree ; and till it hath, why fear the mere playthings of fate? The rain may wet, the tempest rage, the lightning play in antics in yon clouds, but till the word is spoken in tones louder than yon rumbling thunder, Galliano shall bethink him of life, not death!"

Scarce had he spoken, when a broad, bright flash, that, for a moment, lit every thing around brighter than noon-day, struck the spire of the marble-pillar, which had been the concealment of the companions, shivering it in fragments.

"Lo, the warning of the waters!" exclaimed Galliano, pointing to the ruins. But five minutes agone, thou and I were there, for shelter and concealment. Now, behold the wreck of our ark! The lightning hath robbed it of its glory and its power, and we must here bide the peltings of the pitiless storm!"

All was darkness again, and yet the eyes of the two were rivetted in silence, in the direction of the shattered pillar. A dim, hazy light seemed to rise from its centre, like the faint rays of a lamp in some dark passage. The pillar, broken as it was, was still about three feet above the level of the fast rising waters surrounding it. The rain fell ceaselessly, and yet that strange, dim light still shone around the broken remnant of the pillar. Cautiously, the noble and his companion advanced towards the spot. They looked down—the pillar was hollow, and a circular flight of narrow stairs, widening as they descended, met their gaze. A lamp with five burners, was suspended from the ceiling, a small distance from the gap, apparently under the earth. The entrance was not more than five feet, but gradually widened in its descent. The walls were damp, and big drops of vault-sweat were continually falling to the bottom. A low, moaning noise saluted the ears of Galliano and his companion, as they bent their heads and listened. A sickly pallor overspread the features of the latter, and a momentary tremor ran through his frame. He glanced at Galliano, whose face was dimly seen by the reflection of the vault lamp ; but the latter, though gazing thoughtfully at the mysterious entrance, evinced not the slightest symptom of astonishment, or fear.

"What dost think it is?" said Paulo, gathering courage from the other's coolness.

"Think!" answered the noble, with an exulting smile, "think! why, that the elements have revealed to us one of the chief pathways to the dungeons of the 'Ten.' Had we now but twenty men, brave-hearted and true, we might storm this dungeon-entrance, and perhaps rid Venice of its tyrants, without the spilling of more blood than flows in the veins of the death-dealing 'council!' Dost thou not see through it all?" continued Galliano, his face radiating with alternate scorn and pleasure at the discovery ; "dost not see through it all? For safety and escape, should they be assailed in their infernal council, lo! the staircase and the magic outlet! Would they, at midnight, enter, unobserved, their bloody caverns, lo! the marble door! When their fiendish tortures have put to death a victim, lo! the staircase and the door—close beside the canal—by which, at dark hour and solemn, to slide the mutilated corse into the deep lagoon! Who dies in Venice? Who breathes his spirit out, among his kindred, on the calm and peaceful couch of home? We die not—we disappear! and the Adriatic tide of an after day, finds us floating down its current, our bodies crisped and headless—memorials of Blood,

Secret Deed and Tyranny—tyranny that hides its dastard face in God's day-light, and prowls about in darkness, with dagger, cloak, and mask, to sweep from Life and Earth the suspected! The marble door—the secret stair-case—and the grand canal! Convenient instruments! But the red lightning hath shivered their pillar, and we, we the patriotic band, we of the sworn body, shall rend the tyrants themselves!"

Though excited almost to delirium, yet the young noble's voice rose not above the gale.

"Let us depart," said Paulo, looking earnestly around; "eyes, even now, may be upon us! Let us depart!"

"In good faith, not I," replied the noble, coolly; "I go not hence till these eyes know more of the mysteries of yon staircase. Wilt follow me?"

"I have no weapon," answered the gondolier, half fearfully.

"Thy knife?" said Galliano, interrogatively.

"I have it not."

"Then fill thy pockets with scraps of yon strewed marble," said the noble, gaily, and springing into the pillar; "they will, I trow, be weapons enough to silence the clamors of any we may encounter ere our return. Hast got them?"

"I have."

"Stay, a moment, here is my dirk: thou may'st have need of it. Now, as thou hast a heart, follow me!"

The noble drew his oft-tried rapier, and, throwing off his cloak, that it might not interrupt his activity, or speed, quickly, yet cautiously, descended the narrow stairs. The gondolier followed after him, noiselessly as possible, his heart beating painfully with excitement.

CHAPTER VIII.

THE DUNGEONS OF THE TRIBUNAL

AFTER descending the spiral staircase, our heroes, on verging to the right found themselves in a long, broad avenue, of an iron hue, dimly lighted by lamps with three burners, suspended by heavy chains from the ceiling. On either side of the passage were massive oaken doors, covered with heavy iron bars, rivetted transversely, and each fastened outwards by a ponderous padlock. The cells were ranged in pairs,—i. e. every pair formed one little block, or square, which was divided from the next by a narrow pathway leading into the avenue behind it. The passages were covered with a dark, yielding substance, which had the effect of killing the echo of a footfall; so that, while one stood conversing with a companion, a spy might, unheard, turn an angle, and, approaching within earshot, catch every word. The door of each cell was numbered, near the top, immediately under a transversed pair of shoulder-bones, surmounted by a grinning skull—the relics, doubtless, of the cell's last victim. The ceiling of this subterranean vault presented a dark, spongy aspect, as if intended to drown the loudest sound, and thus prevent the groans of the tribunal's victims from being heard above.

The noble, despite his natural nerve, paused and shuddered at the grim silence and appalling aspect of the strange scene. A dreary, heavy, choking atmosphere was around him, and he repented of having thrown away his cloak. Taking a few steps onward, a sudden and unaccountable feeling came over him. The iron of his nerves seemed gradually departing, and the invincible energy and indomitable resolution of his nature, by some mysterious process, appeared to be oozing through his pores, and his blood, weak and tremulous, felt as if converted into water. His cheeks and lips blanched—heavy drops of hot sweat rolled rapidly down his limbs—his eyes grew haggard—his lips quivered—the moisture was fast departing from his gums—his knees smote each other—respiration grew, every moment, more and more difficult, and he felt as if the Icy-Hand were tugging with his frame to tear away his heart. A long, deep, agonising groan fell upon his ear, and, dropping on his hands and knees, his face close to the ground, he crawled, shudderingly, backwards, in the direction of the staircase. His feet touched something heavy behind him, and, turning his face, Galliano beheld his companion stretched upon the pave, his mouth and eyes agape, his erst sun-burnt cheeks pale as chalk, his lips twitching as if a serpent were gnawing them within, his breast heaving with agony, and his arms swinging above his head frantically, as if to ward off some horrid phantom visible to his terrified eyes. With a bold and convulsive effort, the noble passed him, and, weak and faint, reached the base of the staircase. A few moments sojourn there partially recovered him; when, anxious for his companion, and deeming his strength sufficiently restored for the task, he boldly rushed into the passage, and, catching the gondolier by the collar of his jacket, dragged the body, hastily, into the area by the stairs.

The sudden change of atmosphere soon restored the latter to his senses, and re-invigorated the strength of both—yet both were pale, very pale. Their eyes were strained and bloodshot with their recent terror and struggles to escape the empoisoned air.

"We have seen enough—let us now depart," said Paulo, half whisper-ingly.

"Not I," replied Galliano; "life and curiosity are yet sufficiently strong within me, to urge me on to more than a glance at these infernal avenues. I must behold in full, ere I again ascend to the world above us. The atmosphere of the avenues beyond is, perchance, better than that of the first. Did'st notice that it was not till we passed the third block of cells that the air changed so suddenly, and that it was when near the fourth that the deadly ether first saluted us?"

"Methinks I did; but what interference drew you from that?"

"A plain one," replied the noble; "murder is going on in that cell—murder, not by the knife, nor by the pincer, nor by the thumb screw, rack or burning floor—but murder by robbing the poor victim of his feelings and senses one by one, that, with his last gasp, the victim may spring into the portals of Eternity with a thrill of agony unequalled by any other torture. Did'st hear a groan!"

"I did."

"Be sure 'twas the victim's last! No torture could drag from living clay such a groan as that; it, more than the sulphurous air, struck me to my knees!"

"So did it me—I never heard its like."

"Hush!" said Galliano, whisperingly, and placing his finger on his lip.

A sound like the rumbling of a door swinging upon its rusty hinges, now jarred upon their ears. The noble peeped cautiously into the passage, and beheld a sight which made his blood creep. Two stout, goodly sized wretches, garbed in long greasy, blood-stained tunics, without sleeves, and sandalled and capped, were dragging the remains of their victim on a broad board from the cell. The body was entirely naked, and by the process of the torture, reduced almost to a skeleton. The little flesh that remained upon the limbs was torn and ragged, as if by the violent struggles of the victim while writhing under the poisonous and sense-killing vapour. The wretches, after having taken out the body and the vapour box, threw in a powder to kill the effluvia remaining in the cell, carefully locked the door, and taking up the body, slowly and silently disappeared through an adjoining passage.

"The curse of a Venetian be upon ye, bloodhounds!" muttered the young noble, shaking his doubled fist in the direction which they had taken. "Follow me !" he exclaimed, turning suddenly to his companion, and immediately dart-ing into the vault, apparently with the intention of hastening after the murderers, and inflicting upon them the punishment due to their crime.

The noble ran with speed, but soon found himself bewildered in the countless and complicated passages. His sword was drawn, and grasping it firmly in his hand, he darted from avenue to avenue, from narrow passage to narrow passage, his eyes the while, searching every lighted and dark spot for the myrmidons of the tribunal, but all in vain—they had vanished. Tired, panting and spent out, he leaned against a cell, in one of the avenues, for support. Having rested awhile, and bethinking him of his companion, he strode swiftly in, what appeared to him, the direction of the staircase. But in this he was baffled ; for, notwith-standing all his efforts, he could not reach the spot. Avenue after avenue, passage after passage he traversed, but all in vain, and he was forced to trust to chance in reaching it at all.

In this critical situation, and pondering on the dangers to which he was exposed, he resolved to explore every avenue and passage till all the secrets of the vault were known to him, or till he stumbled upon some path leading to an outlet. Accordingly, he paced impatiently the lengthy avenue in which he stood, till he unexpectedly found himself within a few yards of an approaching personage, masked and enveloped in a long, dark mantle. Fortunately for Galliano, his own sombre costume, the sound-killing pave, and the darkness around, prevented him from being seen or heard, and he darted hastily into a side passage, where he overheard a voice demanding of the approaching figure the password.

"The cross of St. Mark's," was the response.

"Pass on," said the voice, in a satisfied tone.

As Galliano was about leaving his concealment, a hand, from some one behind, was laid gently upon his shoulder, and some one whispered into his ear,—

"Stay ! Death is before thee !"

"Ha !" exclaimed the noble, quickly recognising and grasping the hand of the gondolier; "I'm glad I've found thee. I thought thee lost in these infernal labyrinths."

"I have been searching for thee," said the other, in a hollow whisper.

"Knowest thou the direction of the staircase ?" continued Galliano, earnestly, "for I have lost it."

A despairing groan escaped the gondolier, as he replied, "and I, great God !"

"Hush !" exclaimed the noble, quickly, and clapping his hand to his com-panion's mouth, "thou'lt betray us !"

They plunged deeper into the gloomy pass, and stood mute as statues ; when, finding they were not overheard, they stole carefully into the avenue behind, and, after looking watchfully around, walked onward. As they passed on, a masked figure, holding a sharp-pointed spear, suddenly darted from an adjoining passage demanding sternly,—

"The password ?"

"The cross of St. Mark's," replied Galliano, carelessly, and passing on.

"The password, thou ?" said the figure addressing Paulo.

"The cross of St. Mark's,' muttered the gondolier, in a tone, which nothing but the last, bold effort of the despairing could call up.

"Pass on," was the response.

Tremblingly, indeed, did Paulo obey the order, while the sentinel returned silently into the passage from which he had so suddenly emerged.

"Cease thy trembling man," whispered the noble, "else we are ruined ! By chance I learned the watchword, and therefore was prepared for the fellow's challenge. Remember it !"

"I shall ;—"the cross of St. Mark's !"

"Aye ! That knave was a watchman, and challenged us when we passed his post. Be sure we'll meet with others, ere we reach our goal."

"Why not ask the next to lead us to the staircase ?"

"Umph! I doubt if 'twould be safe. He would, for all our knowledge of the password, suspect us. Suspicion would be the forerunner of capture and certain death. No; we must trust to fortune for escape."

"The watchword," cried a figure, suddenly entering the avenue.

They gave it, and passed on with throbbing hearts.

"'Tis a mercy he overheard us not," whispered Galliano; "we must be chary of our speech. These villains must have their allotted posts, like the watchmen of our city. Count the dungeon-sets we pass, ere we again are challenged."

"Six," whispered the gondolier, as soon as they had passed the next sentry.

"Right, my count exactly," said the noble, softly; "could we now, through the dim light of these avenues, but learn the number of dungeon-squares from end to end of the vault, and the number of avenues, we might easily compute the amount of sentries at all times on guard here."

"The advantage of such knowledge?"

"We then might guess the number of foes we should be likely to meet, in case we should storm the 'Ten' in this, their den. I doubt much if their number is as great as the prevailing fears and reports of our countrymen would lead one to imagine. Their great weapons are mystery and fear. Venetians are prone to fear an unseen power, and that is an all-subduing sword when properly handled. And yet, after all how men, gifted with reasoning faculties and brave hearts, can be frightened by such paltry bug-bears is more than I can fathom. A mystery is easily made up by the simplest mind; the lookers on may see the action of the mystery, but the mind that created it sees in't only the working result of his own mechanism; tear away the cover, or the curtain, and the gaping spectators, seeing the machinery, no longer wonder. These dungeons look mysterious and terrible, and yet they are nothing more than thick wooden boards put together by the aid of iron nails and ordinary rivets. The head and bones of some poor victim are nailed upon them, for effect. Take away the human—human? inhuman, rather —instruments, and of what danger can the dumb bones and painted boards be? A frowning, elf-like visage and physique, like to the form and features of the last knave that challenged us, are easily made up by the aid of paint and dirt and black cloth. They might be made on blocks, to frighten children with, and yet the scare-crow would be harmless; so with these knaves on duty here; disrobe them of their black tunics, shave them of their matted beards and lanky wigs, wash them of their stained hands and filthy faces, and what would their bare forms present of terror more than ours? Pah! that men should suffer wrongs, and let the perpetrators pass unpunished, because wrapped in mystery and paint!"

The gondolier acknowledged the truth of these observations, but, though physically brave, he could not shake off the fears which his adventures among the dungeons thus far, had gathered round him.

They passed on, giving the password whenever demanded, till they reached the end of the avenue—but no outlet met their view.

"What shall we do?" cried Paulo, whose presence of mind and courage now seemed to shrink at the hopeless prospect before them.

"Pass on to the next,'" was the cool response.

"But the sentries there may be the same that we have already met," added the gondolier, falteringly.

"We'll make sure they are not, by taking our path to the one beyond. Lo, our goal! see where the light gleams in yon area." continued Galliano, when they, had reached the point proposed, and pointing, as he spoke to what seemed to be the entrance to the staircase.

The hearts of both bounded, as they saw deliverance. They pressed forward hastily, but on reaching the threshold of the area, the cheek of the gondolier blanched as if suddenly converted into marble—they were on the threshold of the hall leading to the council chamber; a sentry was on duty there—almost before them—pacing slowly, up and down the hall. His back was towards them, when they approached so near his post. He was about turning, when a sudden jerk of the gondolier, by the hand of Galliano, preserved both from the eyes of the sentry, as he re-paced the pave by the door.

"Where is thy coolness—where thine eyes, man," muttered the noble, as they hurried into a conti uous and dark passage.

They had been in their concealment scarce a minute, when a cavalier cloaked and masked, and wearing a scarlet cap shaped like a sugar-loaf, which was ornamented by a tall, white feather, fastened by a glittering loop in front, passed them and entered the hall.

"The password?" demanded the sentinel, presenting his spear.

"The mercy of the Ten," responded the cavalier, laughing.

"Pass," said the sentinel, recovering his weapon, and resuming his pace.

"The watchword is changed!" whispered Paulo, aghast.

"Aye, for that department," added the noble, in explanation. "Fear not—another door than the one we entered, must be near at hand as the quick breathing and sudden entrance of yon cavalier plainly denote. Let us seek it."

They emerged slowly from their concealment, and watching the moment when the sentinel had turned, strode hastily past the door. Turning an angle, some few yards beyond, they found themselves in a broad, high arched passage, whose only light was received from a torch, which stood in the centre of the pave, supported by three portable, upraised poles.

"We are near the door," whispered the noble; "dost detect the coolness of the air?"

"I do," responded Paulo, looking fearfully around.

"Have the dagger I gave thee at hand," continued Galliano, "for if there be a pass word for the knave who stands sentry at the door other than the ones we have, we must fight for our egress."

As they proceeded, the passage, at every step grew less wide, till only one person could make his way. A faint light ahead encouraged them, and they trod swiftly on, when all at once, they found themselves in a large, semi-circular vault, lighted by three lamps, hanging by chains from the high arched ceiling, each about forty feet from the other. The atmosphere was cold and refreshing, and contrasted strongly with the confined air of the vault they had just left. A sound like the rushing of waters fell upon their ears, but no human object met their searching eyes. By the light of the burning lamps, they could distinctly perceive a semi-circular range of dungeons before them, each heavily barred and locked. Convinced, by the atmosphere and the noise of the beating surge, that either a door or window was at hand, the keen eye of the noble searched every spot around, till, glancing upwards, over the range behind him, he discovered a small, grated window, through the broken panes of which the night winds rushed, and revealed to him at once the cause of the refreshing atmosphere around him. While pondering on what part of Venice the grated window faced, his companion touched him gently on the shoulder, and pointed silently to a figure, with his back towards them, sitting on a low stool, in the extreme corner of the vault. Imagining, and with reason, that this man must be the sentry of the main entrance though, in consequence of the gloom around him, no door was visible, Galliano touched his lip with his finger, to his companion, and, grasping firmly the hilt of his drawn sword, advanced, on tip-toe, in the direction of the sentry, when he suddenly grasped him by the throat, and hurled him to the ground. It was the work of a moment, and so hastily and perfectly had the feat been executed, that the poor wretch fell without a mutter, or a groan.

"A word, a whisper, or the slightest movement, and this steel is in thy throat!" exclaimed Galliano, in a hurried whisper, as he stood threateningly over the prostrate figure, his sword pointing to his breast.

"Seize his keys!" added the noble, to his companion, who, dagger in hand, had now approached.

Paulo stooped, and, from the girdle of the unresisting sentinel, wrenched a hugh bunch of keys, and handed them, in silence to Galliano, who, grasping them firmly, bade his astonished victim rise. The gondolier assisted, and, in the act, bared his dagger across the wretch's throat, muttering as he did so,—"Attempt to struggle, escape, or call for help, and my knife and thy gullet shall be quickly acquainted!"

The poor wretch made no attempt to disobey, but gazed sullenly at his captors.

"Now, knave," said the young noble, imperatively, "where is the door that eads from these infernal caverns? Speak, or I'll slay thee!"

The sentinel spoke not, but pointed to the wall in front of which he had been sitting.

The noble turned, and discoverd a broad, dark door, with a huge lock and three heavy cross bars. Seizing, instinctively, the largest key, he applied it cautiously to the key-hole, and turned the lock. Then sliding back the bars, the door easily came open, revealing a flight of broad, winding stairs.

"On reaching the top of yon staircase, where shall I find myself?" demanded the noble, sternly.

"In a bare apartment, lit by a single lamp, the door of which, fastened by a single lock, opens into the Grand-square, directly fronting St. Mark's," replied the sentry.

"And that door can be opened from without?"

"Ay—by a latch-key, of which every member of the council is provided with a duplicate. The exterior of the apartment represents an ordinary dwelling, and is guarded on either side by the habitation of a member of the Tribunal."

"Is this the entrance for prisoners?"

"It is."

"The only one?"

"No ;—there is another."

"And that——"

"Is through a secret door in the white pillar by the Rialto."

"How long art thou on guard here?"

"From dusk till dawn."

"Thy name?"

"Ugerto."

"How long hast thou been in the service of the 'Ten?'"

"Three years."

"Stayest thou by force?"

"I do."

"Thy wages?"

"Bread, wine, raiment and couch."

"If thou desert'st?"

"The creatures of the 'Ten' dare not desert."

"And if they do?"

"If caught, the 'Fire Chamber' is their doom—they are burned to a crisp and their ashes flung, at midnight, into the Adriatic."

"Have any prisoners been brought through this door to-night?"

"Ay, two."

"The first——"

"A woman—the daughter of a noble."

"Her name !"

"I know it not."

"Where is she now?"

"In the next range."

"Through yonder passage ?"

"The same."

"And the second victim——"

The sentinel's face grew pale, and his voice husky, as he replied—"A gondolier, I think."

"Ha ! and he—"

"Lies chained in yonder cell—number eight."

"Is the key in this bunch?"

"Ay—the key of every cell in the first range is there."

"And this is the first range?"

"It is."

"The number of ranges in all?"

"Twenty."

"And, of cells, each range counts.——"

"Fifty."

"Stay a moment, till I open number eight."

" Thou can'st not, without my aid. Except by a practised hand, the lock cannot be turned without alarming the bellwatcher in the next range."

" The distance is too far for him to hear."

" Thou dost mistake : to every lock there is a wire attached, that rings a bell in the watch-room, which none but an accustomed turnkey can prevent."

" The motive of that ?"

" 'Tis a safeguard against strange hands, in case a stranger should, by any possility, find entrance here, and seek to set captives free; and also to prevent pribiners from escaping by forcing the doors."

" Wilt thou open number eight?"

" Ay, if thy companion here will take his dagger from across my throat ?"

" Dost know the prisoner in number eight ?"

" I do."

" His name ?"

" Gennaro !"

" Ha ! Didst thou know him ?

" I did !"

" Wert thou of his calling ?"

" Ay, my lord ! I it was who first taught him how to pull the gondolier's oar; taught him how to brave the deep and angry tide when billowy waves ran high amidst the storm. We slept under the same roof, ate at the same table, prayed the same prayers, from his infancy, till I was summoned before the ' Ten.' "

" Indeed ! Who art thou ?"

" Gennaro's father !"

" Ha! his father ? Swear it!"

" As I do hope for Heaven's mercy !"

" Enough; I trust thee ! Release him !"

Paulo let go his hold, and the old sentinel bowed his thanks. Emotion was plainly visible on his boldly delineated features; but it was the emotion of one who had long since learned to curb the rising passions of his heart. His face was livid, clammy; his eyes large, dark, but lustreless; his hands broad, bony, and indicative of great strength; his form about the common height, his shoulders broad, and covered with a loose, coarse, dark-hued tunic, which reached but slightly below his knees, revealing the nakedness of his legs and feet, the latter being preserved from contract with the ground by a pair of rough, black sandals. His arms were bare, and his chin and upper lip covered with a profusion of dark bushy hair. His aspect was hideous, gaunt, and grim. As the light of the hanging lamp fell upon his face, the keen eye of Galliano detected a twitching on his wrinkled brow and cheeks, and a swimming in his lustreless eyes, which plainly told how deeply his heart was wrung with suffering.

" Shall I open number eight ?" asked the sentry, his voice thicker and hoarser than before.

" Thou meanst no treachery ? '

" By all my hopes of Heaven, no !"

"Enough—I'll trust thee. Take the keys."

The old man took the bunch, and, selecting the proper key, advanced towards the dungeon. After cautiously turning the lock and shoving back the bars, the door swung open, and the old man entered the cell. A noise, like the falling of chains, was heard, and, a few moments afterwards, the old man reappeared, bearing in his sinewy arms the slumbering body of his son. He laid his burden softly upon the pave before the noble; and, kneeling by it, pointed to the body and exclaimed, in a low, choked voice,—

" Behold, in the dungeons of the masters and rulers of Venice—behold a sight for a father !"

" Hast thou a father's heart and permittest thy son to lie there, when an effort of thine could restore him to life and freedom?" said Galliano, in a stern, reproachful tone, eying the sentry.

"That effort were death to him and me," responded the old man, in a low, hoarse voice ; " the argus-eyed Tribunal would hunt us in the extreme corners of the earth, and drag us back to unescaping death!"

" What ! lovest thou life ?"

"Ay, count—for my boy's sake."

"His sake ! Ha! ha! old man, what aid canst thou render him ?"

"None, my lord, till his sentence be o'er. Then——"

" Ha ! and then ?"

" Then,—that is my secret, my lord !" said the sentry, suddenly recollecting himself, and raising the body. " Follow me, and thou shalt see," he added, lifting his son carefully, and walking in the direction of the passage through which the noble and his companion had come.

"Ha! stay, whither goest thou ?" demanded Galliano, sternly, and advancing towards him.

The sentry answered not, but on reaching the entrance to the passage, paused, and pressing a stone, a door in the wall flew open, into which the old mn entered cautiously, Galliano and his companion following, wonderingly.

The apartment into which they entered was square, about six feet in height, and the same in length and width. A small lamp rested on a low cross-legged table, which stood in the furthest corner, beside a bed. It was a wretched, filthy-looking hole, and the poisonous stench arising from the bed was almost sufficient to strangle the noble.

Having entered, the sentry placed his senseless son upon the rude couch, and then carefully and silently closed the door. A bolt soon made the latter fast, and the old man, though really deeply agitated, seated himself coolly upon the foot of the bed, and gave a loud laugh.

" How now—the meaning of this ?" demanded the noble, a suspicion of treachery flashing across his mind.

" Let me have my laugh, my lord," said the sentry calmly. " No living soul, ourselves excepted, is aware of the existence of this chamber. It is the handiwork of these unpractised hands, and made during the few hours allotted to me for sleep. I have robbed nature of her dues to cheat the eyes and interests of men. It is a rare workmanship, is it not, my lord ?" he added, with a chuckle and a smile which gave him more the semblance of a demon than a man. " Look, my lord, how tastefully the hangings and the tapestry are arranged." As he spoke, he touched a cord beside the foot of the couch, when, as if by magic, the sombreness of the walls changed to a beautiful and luxurious appearance, each side having a portrait in its centre. The ceiling was as white as porphyry, and a number of circles, each smaller than the other, were painted with great skill, in its centre, giving it the appearance of a magnificient dome. The table, by some mysterious process, assumed the aspect of a card-board, and the low couch became a couch of rare beauty. The floor alone remained unchanged, and its dark hue presented a melancholy contrast with the rest of the apartment.

The noble and his companion were mute with astonishment. The former at last broke the silence, by demanding of the sentry—" Art thou man, or devil ?"

" Neither, my gracious lord," replied the sentry, with a sardonic grin, " nor magician, nor fiend ; but a simple man, one who has made use of his simple wits to outwit the craftiest ones of Venice."

" The Tribunal ?"

" The same, my lord. For years, they have played upon each nerve of this poor frame, till they have broken—as they think—the sole remaining links that bind me to man. As a captive and a slave, they have used me as they listed. As a captive and a slave, I used what they could not succeed in robbing me of, my will, to their ultimate undoing. Behold !"

As he spoke, the sentry touched a spring in the picture, when the latter fell back, revealing a large, high-vaulted chamber, faintly lighted. The room was bare of furniture or ornament, of any kind, and nothing but a single lamp suspended from the ceiling could be descried.

" The purpose of that chamber ?" said Galliano, interrogatively.

" 'Tis the dungeon into which they are plunged who are doomed by the Tribunal to linger out a torturing life by starvation," answered the sentinel, coolly. " But it is not used much," he continued, ironically ; " the ' Ten' are rapacious, and love to hear the quick groans and screams and yells of those whom they doom. But see, my boy moves ; the air has changed the action of his blood. In a few moments he will be conscious, and then ye must all depart ; for the dawn is close at hand. But not a word must he hear from you that will teach him who I am !"

" But if I should wish to return, say by to-morrow night—with a friend or two with me—wilt thou admit us ?" asked Galliano.

" I will," replied the sentry, " but remember and ponder on the peril of the attempt."

" I shall remember all," said the noble, " and the Tribunal shall remember me too ; I have a work to do, old man—a work in which five thousand of the bravest and most patriotic of Venetians are sworn to aid me—a work, I say—a work of retribution—dost thou understand me ?"

Their eyes met—and, though neither uttered a word, they understood each other's thoughts and meanings, and were satisfied with each other's faith.

" Ha ! where am I ?" cried the gondolier, starting from the couch, and gazing around him with astonishment. " Sure I know your faces !" he added, gazing alternately at the noble and his companion. " Are ye what ye seem—or are ye but the dreamy figures of my crazed brain. Speak ; art thou not Paulo, the son of the fruit-vender."

" I am, Gennaro," replied Paulo, in a low tone extending his hand.

" And thou?" he gazed, addressing the noble.

" Thy friend," said Galliano, softly; " but one whose name not even these walls must hear. Thou art a freeman, once more, if thou hast strength to walk to where I'll hide thee even from the Tribunal. What sayst thou—be brief in thy answer, man, for day is fast approaching."

" I cannot walk," replied Gennaro, faintly, and sinking on the bed, " my limbs have lost their wonted strength. I am feebler than a child."

" Let him remain," said the sentry in a choked tone, which he endeavoured to hide by coughing. " Let him remain, then, in Heaven's name. I'll answer for his safety with my life. His trial cannot take place till to-morrow night, at the earliest, as the Tribunal sit only at night—and, as other prisoners are yet to be tried, ere he is summoned, he shall in thy company depart, I trust never to return·"

" Then farewell," said the noble, extending his hand to the prisoner. " The Tribunal, perchance, did Venice a service in arresting thee. Thou hast a foretaste of the horrors that have been rioting in these infernal caverns; it will serve to nerve thee for the coming trial. Brother, farewell."

A moment more, and the gondolier was alone. But a few minutes had elapsed when the sentry again entered the apartment.

" Thou must return to thy dungeon," said he in a low deep tone. " There is danger that thy cell may be searched between this and the coming night, and if in such case, thou were not found, my life would answer for thine absence. Thou wilt receive no food during thy imprisonment ; therefore take this loaf and pitcher of wine—all I can give thee—and when the hour of ten arrives, be sure that I shall be with thee. Follow me in silence ; for thy life or death dependeth on thy conduct. Follow me."

Without a word, without a murmur, though with his brain full of conjectures, the young man soon found himself re-locked in his first dungeon.

CHAPTER IX.

THE HOUSE OF THE USURER.

WITH our kind reader's leave, we will now leap over time a week, during which interregnum some instances pertaining to this history transpired, which in their proper time and place shall find a fitting record. We'll change the scene, too, and usher into sight one fair being whom we have already kept too far in the vista—our herione.

Reader, hast thou ever been in the favoured land—the land of song and beauty; the land, above all others, where the Eternal One tarried the longest while creating his fair and beauteous earth—the land where every zephyr is an angel's whisper—where every rustling of a flower leaf is a flower's sigh—where the orange blooms with a moistening, golden beauty that almost shames the bright and mellowing sun—where the dews of dawn infuse new life, new strength, new blood, new nerve, into the weariest frame—where the pale cheek is made rosy and healthful as the first blush of youth, by the pellucid atmosphere—where, at night, the stars shine brightest, and the moon gleams purest—where the sky is bluer, the clouds lovelier, the atmosphere clearer, the flowers brighter, gayer, and more lovely in their variegated hues, and the waters more blue and clear than in any other of the water-bound islets of God's fair garden, earth—where man is blithest, gayest, boldest—where woman is more the seraph, and—at the same time syren, the syren conscious of the all-conquering attributes of her nature—where old men of three-score are glad, joyous, and fleet-limbed as the youth of eighteen of less-favoured climes—where every gale hath music in it—where the very waves dash on the pale sands like murmuring lullabys, and are echoed by the busy, everflying zephyrs above—and where the full, loud, ripe, hearty laugh is heard from every honest heart, the isle around, for very mirth and gladness—Venice? Hast thou been there, reader mine, and not felt thyself nearer the Paradise of eastern fable, or that truer, holier home spoken of in the Tome of Tomes, than ever, in reality, or in thy dreams before? What though dark dungeons and bridges, and narrow winding waters, confront thee at every turn; what though mystic tales, and legends of terror and mystery, salute thine ear at dawn, high noon, and dusk, and even; what though grim processions, and fiendish instruments of a power inhuman, warn thee to be mute in thy speech and thought, and ever inert in action; what then? The calm, refreshing, invigorating air; the mellow haze, and inspiriting sheen, of earth's day-god; the bright blue sky; the deep, broad, gay, sun-kissed mirror of the clouds and sky; the Adriatic; are about thee still, telling thee of beauties so vast and glorious, that man, for all his powers of appreciation of the bright and beautiful—for all his scepticism of the works of the Deity—for all his loathing of the depravity of man—must first bow his head in worship to the bright and beautiful, ere he passes censure on the things of ill and villany around him.

In an obscure quarter of the city, in a dwelling as humble in its exterior as the obscurity of the section in which it stood, dwelt Uberoni, the usurer. Though strongly suspected of possessing wealth, the humble exterior of his abode seemed to give such belief the lie. Though as well known throughout Venice as the Doge himself, and equally as loathed, yet, for all his reputation for wealth, no man's doors were freer from the depredations of midnight thieves, nor the person of Foscari himself more safe from danger or insult. In fact, he was strongly suspected of being one of the numerous instruments, or spies, of the secret and dreaded Tribunal, and by not a few was he secretly deemed to hold a more important position in the eyes of that terrible body. Though the quarter of the town in which he lived was inhabited by the poorest and vilest, and therefore the section most populated, still for years previous to the opening of our tale, the rude, low dwellings on either side of the usurer's house, had stood tenantless. Though their rents were, comparatively, nominal, still so great and so universal was the dread of this man, that the dwellings in question were shunned by all, as if a curse rested upon them. Whenever the usurer was seen to leave his door, at what hour soever of the day or night, the inhabitants of the street, though sitting before their own doors, ceased speaking —the laugh was broken—the merry jest sundered—the low whisper silenced, each eye bent fearfully to the ground, till he had passed from their sight. His door was ever closed and locked, and his small windows heavily curtained—precautions almost entirely useless; for scarcely a being, of the thousands dwelling in that part of the city, passing, would have had the nerve to turn his eye in the direction of the house, though its door stood agape. A small, square, faded sign hung by the entrance, giving notice of the name and calling of the tenant, and also of his business hours; still, as was well known to the people of that neighbourhood, the usurer did his business elsewhere.

On a bright morning, about a week after the incidents recorded in the preceding chapter, a young, handsome, and gaily-attired cavalier was seen advancing in the direction of the usurer's house. He wore scarlet trousers, fitting tightly to the skin, the outward seams hidden by a bright, gold-spangled stripe; a jacket, of blue velvet, trimmed with white ermine and snowy frills, and a jewelled cross; a shoulder cloak, of the same glossy material; a circular, low-crowned cap, of a hue corresponding with his cloak and jacket, ornamented with a high, ostrich plume, fastened in front by a jewelled loop; white kid gauntlets, yellow boots, and a long slender, silver-burnished rapier. His figure was slightly above the common height, and finely moulded, his step firm and proud, his features of the Roman order, and haughty as the noblest-born of that once martial race; his head was covered with hair of the deepest jet, and was thrown backwards in ringletted masses, revealing in full his broad, highly-polished brow; he wore small moustaches, and his jetty beard was trimmed to a point. His whole appearance at once proclaimed his rank, and as he passed, the obsequious and deferential bows and doffing of caps, by the people, attested their knowledge of his name, caste, and person. On arriving at the house of the usurer, the young noble tapped hastily at the door. It was opened slowly by a tall, stout black, dressed in a long, dark tunic, fastened together, in rough, careless folds, round the waist, by a leathern belt, from which hung a long slender dagger, encased in a sheath of plain brass; a pair of well-worn sandals completed his attire.

"Is thy master at home, knave?" demanded the noble, haughtily.

The black answered by gestures that he was, but engaged.

"But I must see him," said the noble, brushing past him haughtily, and entering a door on his right.

The black gave a significant shrug, closed the door, and disappeared hastily down the basement stairs.

"Ho, ho, my trusty man-of-gold," cried the noble, laughing, on entering the room, as he caught a glimpse of a female dress hastily disappearing through the door of an inner room. "Ho, ho so thou hast not forgot thy young years yet—a petticoat in thy house! Ho, ho! a precious sage and moralist thou art, my trusty grey-beard!"

The usurer coloured, and was stammering an excuse, when the noble, laughing, interrupted him, saying,—

"Nay, no excuses; bring in the lady—I must see her—you know how fond I am of the fair—what pains I take to make myself agreeable, and how agreeable I can make myself when I try. So oblige me with an introduction."

"Pardon me, my lord," said the usurer, slowly, "but I cannot oblige you, at least to-day."

"Why not, my youthful money-lender?" inquired the other, laughing; "you must have the poor thing imprisoned in this little box, like a captive bird, and allow no eyes other than your own, and that dumb porter's and knave of all-work of thine, to gaze upon her beauty, or listen to her songs! And that, too, while Leonardo Foscari—'the Prince of Gay Gallants'—as his companions term him, lives! Out on the—the very idea is unworthy thy reverend wisdom!"

"I'm sorry for it, my lord," replied the usurer, coldly.

"Nay, man, never purse thy brow so deeply," added the noble; "it is bad for thy wrinkles—it exposes them terribly, believe me. Come, my gay Adonis, do let me have one word with—one glimpse of thy Venus!"

"Not to-day, my lord," was the cool response.

"What! you won't? Ha! ha! ha! By St. Mark, I do believe thou hast been cutting thy stale bachelorship, and that this is thy honeymoon! Well, if thou art already jealous, Heaven watch o'er thy young bride, for she'll have a time of it, with thee for her lord! Come, lend me a hundred ducats, and I'll leave thee to thy fair one!"

"A hundred ducats, my lord?"

"Ay, my young bridegroom, a hundred ducats! Not a moiety less will answer."

"But it is impossible, my lord."

"What is impossible?"

"For me to lend you a hundred ducats, my lord?"

"Why so—eh?"

"I have not so much money in the house, my lord."

"Pooh—pooh! fiddlestick! I know your old excuse to drag out of me a higher interest than usual. But it won't do, my venerable child. I must have the money, and instantly—my honour is pledged for it.'

"But your lordship has had three hundred ducats within this fortnight."

"His lordship is perfectly aware of the fact, and his lordship now wishes another hundred added to the amount, and that without delay, as his lordship feels himself growing more and more choleric," added the noble, in a tone not to be misunderstood.

"But I have not the money," said the usurer, biting his lip; "but I might possibly raise it of a friend, if I could give him a pawn for security."

"Nay, but thou'lt raise it without security other than what thou hast had on the other three hundred," said the noble, playing with the hilt of his sword.

"But——"

"Nay, no buts for me," said the noble, laughing, but his pale visage giving the lie to his seeming pleasantness. "I want the money, or I know a tale shall jeopardise thy head."

"My lord," gasped the usurer, turning pale, and starting.

"Ho, ho! it brings thy pale liver up, does it?" said the noble, with a quiet smile of triumph. "I thought it would."

At this moment a groan was heard. The noble started, and looked wonderingly around; when he again turned, he beheld the usurer lying upon the floor, his eyes turned upwards as if in death, and his thin lips covered with white foam.

Somewhat startled, and still more confused, the young noble instantly resolved to quit the house, and return towards evening for the money which he needed. So, summoning the black, and pointing out to the slave the condition of his master, he, with hasty strides, took his departure.

"Ho, ho!" he muttered, as he passed up the street, "how soon that hint of the murder of old Galliano brought him to his senses. The pale fool thought it was forgotten. But he laboured under a mis ake. That is my hold upon his purse and services—when he fails me in either when he dares again to look me so boldly and insolently in the face—the base murder of his white-haired victim, the noble Galliano, shall be a luxurious end to the one I have in store for him. Ha, ha, ha! And then, when I have eased him of his saucy blood, how easy it will be, with a troop of disguised and masked confederates, to enter his crib at night, and take possession of his strong box. Ha, ha, ha! The thought is quite refreshing. But that groan—what could it mean? Spirits hide not themselves in holes and corners by day. So our worthy confessors tell us, and they, passing their days and nights in holy and spiritual studies, should know. And the mysterious petticoat, too—I must understand it, and that before long. Umph!"

And in this singular train of thought—this mingling of the assassin with the rogue—he hied him to the house of a companion.

When the usurer recovered from his spasm, which he did in about half an hour, he found himself stretched on a low, broad, cushioned bench, his head supported by a high pillow. A young girl, of some eighteen or nineteen years, sat on a low bench beside him, wiping, with her handkerchief, the saliva from his lips, and the cold moisture from his cheeks and brow. The stony eyes of the usurer fell on her fair, small, tanned features, and rested there in silence. She was small

In stature, but of a contour of form and features that would strike a sculptor with reverence and awe. Her lips were small, but shaped like a perfect bow, and were ripe and rosy as the flower that, itself the loveliest, reins queen amid the fairest. Her brow was high, but, like the rest of her skin, bronzed by her Italian sun. Her hair, parted in the centre of her forehead, and falling in heavy masses round her neck, was dark and silky as the wings of a raven. Her attire was plain, but

No. 5.

tasty, and revealed in full the perfection of her *petite* figure.   It consisted of a dark merino frock, fitting close to the shoulders and waist, and reaching a little below the knees, while her small and delicately-shaped feet and ankles were encased in black silk stockings, and buskins of the same hue.   She was pale, and the expression of her large dark eyes, as they met the usurer's, was,—

"Thou poor, suffering man, I can feel for thee; for I, too, am a sufferer.''

The usurer interpreted the glance, and the hard stoniness of his eyes immediately changed into a moistening softness that, it was evident, was unusual to them.   Finding this sudden change was visible to the young girl, and fearing that it might be seized by her for a purpose which would conflict with his interest, the usurer coughed to hide his feelings, and finding himself fully equal to the effort, started up with a brief "thanks!" and hastily left the room.

Scarcely had he quitted the apartment, when a hand from without, pushed by the curtain, and a small piece of parchment was thrown into the room.   The young girl picked it up, but ere she had time to read, the footstep of the usurer was heard, and in another moment he was before her. Agitation marked his step and his features, though he was evidently struggling to master it.   He paced the room hurriedly, his eyes bent upon the matting covering the floor.   Finding himself a little calmer, he seated himself upon the cushioned bench, and looking the young girl full in the eyes, said, sternly,—

"Girl of a blighted name, for thy kindness in tending me in my weakness, accept my thanks; in return, if I can do aught for thee, name it.''

"Restore me to my friends," said the girl, falteringly.

The usurer smiled, and shook his head, as he replied,—

"Thy friends cannot receive thee.''

"Have they refused to ?'' asked the young girl, weeping.

"They have not," replied the usurer, "they would be glad, doubtless, to hav thee with them.   Shall I tell thee a secret? and if so, wilt thou retain it ?''

"I ?"   She laughed, but a sob was mingled with it.

"Thou'rt right," said the usurer, catching the meaning of her laugh; "if thou hast no means of conversing, to whom canst thou reveal ?   Thou'rt right; and for that reason I will tell thee why thy friends cannot receive thee—they are not in Venice.''

"No ?''

"No.''

"But where, then ?''

"That remains a mystery.''

"Have they fled?''

"By some strange means, they have," replied the usurer, "but their flight is merely momentary, they will soon return.''

"Thank Heaven for that !''

"They would scarce thank thee for such offering.''

"Ha !''

"When they return—as return they must, they bu return to die !''

"Are they then condemned ?''

"The suspected in Venice are condemn before they are arrested.   The arrest is but the forerunner of the shroud.''

"But they've escaped ?''

"Aye—and I will tell thee how.   Dost remember the night of the old man's arrest ?"

"I do"

"That night Odo, the Tribunal's Death Messenger, presented the old lord a packet; it summoned him to leave undone whatever he was doing—if eating his food, to lay down the untasted mouthful—if drinking, to set down the cup, without tasting, though it were within a hair of his lip—if preparing for his bed, to don his cloak and cap, and, without a word, or a glance, without a movement, without saign which could be translated by a child, to follow the Tribunal's messenger.

He did so; for his rank's sake, the "Ten" awaited his coming. Sooner even than they thought, sooner than they looked for, their victim was before them. Sooner than he wished, the old man stood in the council chamber, in the presence of those whose fiat was as relentless as their decrees were terrible. In a chamber eighteen feet high, fifty broad, and fifty deep, the walls and ceiling hung with black, with devices of every torture used, curiously wrought thereon, each device being in itself a picture to fright the prisoner ere he has spoke a word, ere a word had been spoken to him,—with ten masked men, in black, sitting in a semi-circle, on a raised platform, before him,—pale, but firm, the lord stood before his dooms-men. The charge of endeavouring to suborne the peace and welfare of the state was put against him. The old man replied by demanding the name of his accuser. "Leonardo Foscari," was the answer. The accuser and the accused stood face to face—a triumph in the young man's eyes,—astonishment, withering scorn and defiance, in the face of the old. Deep silence reigned awhile. A sign was given—a box was handed round—the box was opened—and lo! 'twas empty—the lord's doom was spoken, sealed, without a word—the interior of the box was black—nothing whitened it—he was doomed. Three nights afterward he suffered in the sulphur-dungeon. Hast thou ever heard how terrible is that death? I'll tell thee. The victim's dungeon is strongly barred, so that his strength, be it as superhuman as it may, cannot burst the door; the walls and ceiling are covered with soft, springy wool, so that, when frantic, the victim cannot dash his brains out; by degrees, the sulphur, mixed with white powder, ground from lilies' hearts, begins to ooze through holes in the floor: the sensation is delightful beyond conception—to the aged victim youth seems to be restored; the bright visions and dreams of boyhood glide past the mind's eye—the air-built castles, the amours, and gaieties and enjoyment of body and mind pass, as in a mirror, before his mental vision—in a moment, as if by magic, this vanishes, and the victim is seized with cramps and chills—his very blood seems dried up—his veins and nerves knock one against the other, creating pains and agony beyond belief. The flood of vapour changes, as to a mist—through which the victim's countless actions and scenes, from youth to the silver hairs upon his head, the gay and the grave, the innocent and the guilty hours of pastime—it seems as if all the chambers of memory are open wide, that the spectres of the brain are dancing before your eye, as in a magician's mirror. The vapour fades slowly—and again the chills and pains of torture seize upon the victim, only more intensely than before. A sharp pang fastens on his forehead—vultures appear to be devouring his body—he strives to speak, to cry, to groan, but cannot—the pain is so intense that he cannot utter a single word. Again the vapour rises—the victim feels relief according as the mist increases in thickness around him. The cell becomes more crowded with the vapour every moment, and in proportion does the delight of the victim increase. The spiritual world is opened to his mental vision, all his conceptions of the happy land of the hereafter are embodied and figured before him. A spirit stands on the shore, and beckons him to come. The vapour again vanishes, and the former tortures seize him with increasing virulence. He yells, screams, starts, springs from corner to corner of his cell, as if pursued by a demon. Again the vapuor rushes through the floor—the cell becomes hot as fire—the Burning Lake with all its horrors, rises to his view—the King of the Doomed leaves his throne to drag him into his fire—the sweat rushes in torrents from the victim—his senses leave him one by one, and with a cry, rising from the exquisite perfection and very acme of human torture, he bounds into the air. The power of the vapour ceases—the executioner enters the cell, and naught is visible but a mass of fleshless bones."

The orange girl did not shudder—she did not scream—but leaning back in her chair, gazed wonderingly at the speaker. Her features, indeed, changed, and, as the usurer paused, turned, shade by shade, paler and paler, till her whole visage resembled a countenance of cold and frigid marble.

Having exhausted his anger, and indifferent to the terrified feelings of his victim, the usurer changed his tone, and added, in a bland voice—"Time presses—I must hence. When my business for the day is finished, I shall return. Meanwhile ponder on what I have said. If I find thee in a humour consorting with mine own, thy future days shall be one eternal reign of joy and bliss. If not—mark me: the wretch that lives in caverns, and feeds on mouldy diet—whose loathsome carcass even worms shudder at and shrink from—whose bowels, like the fabled magi's, are ever being devoured by serpents—whose palate, like those of the doomed in the ever-flaming lake of the Eternities, is hollow and painful through thirst—I sell thee, girl, the sufferings of such an one shall be bliss, compared with the torsures I have in store for thee! Adieu!"

A minute more, and the orange girl was alone.

Reader, mine, hast thou ever had thy mind so begirt with fears—so harrowed, narrowed, cornered—so hemmed round that the very physical members have seemed to join in the dreadful league against thee—so crushed, so overburdened, so wrought upon by those possessing power over thee, that even the fountains of thy soul have refused thee a single drop of moisture—a single tear—wherewith to cool the fire of thine anguish? Hast thou ever? If not, then kneel, and thank thy God for sparing thee—when others are afflicted—from such heart burning woe.

How still she sat—how calm—how pale—how silent!

The hum of voices spread through the key-hole of the outer door—through the crevices in the crazy walls, and yet no sign, no token that the tenant of that little chamber lived and breathed was visible. There she sat, moveless as marble—her eye gazing on the spot where the usurer last had stood, as if unconscious of the absence of him she had seen standing there!

Dusk had stolen in—lightly at first—then heavier—even as grey hairs fall on the crown of man—until night had usurped the place of day. Night, with her stars and drapery, and clouds, and bright silver orb—night, fair and graceful and beautiful, without—night, all dark, and dreary, and cheerless within.

She moved not, that beautiful, that terrified girl.

The hours waxed on, and yet the usurer, contrary to his word, did not make his appearance. Did his victim expect him—did she yearn for his arrival?

Midnight arrived—midnight: that hour when deeds unholy and dark and murderous are perpetrated by God-defying hands; that hour when the student's brightest conceptions flash athwart his vision,—when man ponders deepest on human schemes, and woman's dreams are holiest—midnight!

The outer door swung back on its oiled hinges, noiselessly—the door of the chamber in which the orange girl sat, opened softly—a hand was laid upon her shoulder; the fear-spell was broken, and, without uttering a moan, or a sob, or a shriek, the orange girl turned her head slightly around. The unknown, at that moment, pulled aside the heavy drapery curtaining the window, when like a bright haze, the sheen of the moon fell upon her features, and the stranger beheld a fair, pale face, gazing at him, her eyes full and lustrous, and tears rushing, like a silent stream, adown her alabaster cheeks.

"Dost thou not know me?" said the stranger, in a low, deep voice.

"Know thee!" she repeated.

"Aye, thou poor, wronged girl," added the stranger, "Dost thou not know me? I am thy friend."

"Friend—my friend!"

"Even thine, Eugenia. Cheer up—I've come to save thee!"

"Save me!"

"Aye, girl! The hour is propitious—the usurer is absent—my gondola is at hand—and friends, who have mourned over thine absence, anxiously look for thee."

"Friends—I'm to sleep in the vault below us—over a dead man's grave—over the ashes of the father of one who—"

"Why dost thou pause, fair one?"

"Thou'lt betray me!" said the girl, timidly.

" Nay," replied the unknown, encouragingy, " I am no s'

" Art sure?"

" Nay, look into mine eyes."

" They are no index of the man."

" Wilt thou not trust me, then ?"

" I trusted once—and was deceived."

" All men are not villains, lovely one."

" Right—my brother was not—nor yet my faher—nor Gennaro—yet al deserted me."

" 'Twas cruel in them.

" It was, and yet they did it. A wronged, betrayed, affrighted girl, I fled from home, and they never tried to find out and bring me back. I fled, to escape reproach, expecting that they would seek me out, promise to chide no more, and take me home."

" And for that thou didst fly thine own home, thy friends, and kin ?"

" For that, and no other."

" Poor girl !"

" I like thee, stranger, thou hast a heart; for lo ! how thy voice doth change while thou speakest. Bend low thine ear, and I will tell thee the name of him over whose grave I am to sleep and dream, till I have dreamt my soul away."

The stranger obeyed. She whispered to him a word—but one—and, almcst ere its final accents died upon her tongue, the chamber echoed with loud, wild, and thrilling laughter.

" Ha, ha, ha ! My father's ! Are circumstances and my suspicions at last verified? Ha, ha, ha ! And am I in the house whose walls do hide his ashes ? Ha, ha, ha ! My father's grave found at last—his murderer, too ! Ha, ha, ha ! Revenge, revenge, thou at last hast found out thine altar !"

He paced the apartment wildly, his brows knit, his cheeks pale, his hand clenching the hilt of his oft-tried blade ; then, turning to the trembling girl, he cried,—

" But thou, poor victim of a coward's lust, and an assassin's tyranny, thou mus hence ! I've pledged my honour to rescue and restore thee to those who, like thyself, have felt the hand of a villain. Nay, fear not—give me thy waist, girl. Time presses, and we must fly, while yet the tiger is absent from his lair."

Throwing his arm around her waist, and raising her like a feather from the ground, he was about rushing with his burden from the apartment, when his ear caught the sound of heavy and hurried footsteps, and the next moment the gigantic black mute stood on the threshold of the door, his left hand holding a burning torch, in his right a naked scimitar, while round his lips, and in his large sleepy-looking eyes, there hovered a grin that would have answered for the chuckle of a fiend.

The aspect of this personage was so revolting, that Galliano, despite his natural nerve, shuddered as his eye fell upon him. The orange girl crept closer and closer to the noble, twiuing her arms tightly round his well-shaped neck, and gazed fearfully upon the hideous being before her.

Conquering his momentary terror, and clasping firmer his burthen, the noble demanded, sternly,—

" Thy business, slave !"

The black raised his large dark eyes, and, pantomimically, ordered him to set his burthen down and depart.

The noble, now wholly self-possessed, laughingly responded, " What if I obey not ?'

The black glanced significantly at his scimitar.

" Ah ! thou wilt make that acquainted with my breast ?"

The mute bowed.

" Thou art very kind, my prince of spades ; but, as I'm in no humour for jesting, I'll e'en disobey thee for the nonce. So give way, or I'll cleave thee to the head."

The mute replied only by planting the spear-pointed torch in the floor of the ball, and casti g on the noble a look of stern defiance.

"What!" cried the noble, sharply, "thou lovest sword-play? Then taste the temper of mine;" and he aimed a hasty blow at the head of the black, which was as quickly parried as given. A cold, heavy laugh warned the noble that he had no mean swordsman to deal with, and, setting his burthen on a chair, he firmly, yet cautiously, reapproached his antagonist in the hall. Their swords met, but so perfect was each in the art of handling his weapon, that neither could touch the flesh of his foe. At every thrust, the black warded off the glittering blade, with a derisive grin that called up all the pride and passion of the noble. Every trick of fence, every stratagem calculated to take away the other's guard, was resorted to, but without success—the black appeared invulnerable. On his part, the mute tried every move to bring his antagonist to disadvantage, but his efforts were vain—victory stood poised between them, not knowing the brow her garland yet should crown.

Through the door the orange girl beheld the combat, which was to restore her to light and liberty, or plunge her deeper into misery. Told she not, in voiceless numbers, prayers to the Mighty One?

The combatants paused spontaneously, as if to recover the muscularity of nerve spent in the all but silent trial.

Lo! hand to hand, foot to foot, eye to eye, they are again. Every nerve is strained, every trick of fence again played o'er. Now, they thrust high—now low—now, round and round, like rings of glittering steel dancing in the air, play their swords. O'er head and shoulders—at breast and neck, they at each other aim. Mark well their eyes—how full, how fiery, how lustrous, and yet how cautious, as if all the daring and cunning attributes of their natures were centred in their eyes!

Again they pause.

Their eyes shoot fire and hate—their breasts swell with loathing and scorn which only those men feel who have a foe, yet know they cannot harm him, because his courage and cunning are, at any moment, a full match for theirs.

Now, they eye each other doggedly, as if conscious that the third trial is victory to one, death to the other, or, perchance, death to both. Shrink they?

Mark the pale cheek—the clasped hands, the anxious eyes of that poor, peril-girt girl within, as they are rivetted upon the features of her champion! Move not her lips? Performs she not a double task? Prays she not, and watches she not?

Lo! their blades are crossed again—quicker than before each weapon flies from point to point—who wavers? Both—they scarce can stand the fire and deadliness of each other's eyes! Death stands between them—his shaft raised on high to strike! Who wavers now, in that struggle! See! the white foam gathers round her lips—now, 'tis changed to blood! Hark! a cry from within—has her champion received the javelin? No: for look, where, across the threshold, lies the black, and where, above him, his knee upon his enemy's breast, the noble's bold hand presses the hilt of that unfailing steel whose point now pins the dark slave to the earth!

Hark! the lock turns in the outer door—the door swings back—and now, the murderer and the first born of the murdered one stand eye to eye, in the presence of the dying, yea, over the sepulchre of the dead!

Mark! how blanches the one cheek—how fires up the other. Note the quailing of the old man's eye, and mark how each white hair rises erect upon his crown, as if in judgment against the owner of the crown—as if conscious that God's human avenger stands there, with bold hand, good sword and unflinching heart, to stain each snowy lock with its owner's blood! The old man, brave in youth, brave in manhood, yea, to his heart's core fearless, why shrinks he now at the eagle eye of one so much in years his junior? He sees his foe before him, yet has not thought enough to reach from its scabbard his sword! Fresh from halls where human blood and dying groans are a nightly banquet—where among the heartless he is the most heartless—old man! old man! where is thy iron heart now?

"Reach forth thy weapon, man," cried Galliano, sternly; "I've sworn to take the life of my father's murderer. Yet would I give thee a chance for the retaining of thy life. Draw, and defend thyself."

The spell was broken—though returned, and the usurer, casting a glance behind him, snatched up the torch, and darted down the stairs leading to the vault. With a spring blithe as his own, the noble darted after him, closely followed by the affrighted orange girl. As she flew past the distended black, a hasty hand attempted to grasp the skirt of her dress, but fear winged her footsteps, and she escaped the death-clutch of the wounded mute.

The vault into which the usurer fled was deep and spacious, and contained a range of nine low arches, which were covered by heavy oaken doors—the depositories, doubtless, of the old man's valuables and papers. The walls were thick and, mouldy, and a chilly atmosphere pervaded its length and breadth. A small blind grating stood on one side of the vault, near the ceiling, while directly beneath it rose an earthy mound, shaped like a lowly grave.

As the orange girl reached the foot of the rough, broad stairs of the vault, she started on beholding Galliano grasping the distended usurer by the throat, with one hand, and with the other pointing to the grave.

The features of the usurer were pale as ashes, his eyes seemed starting from their sockets, and his whole frame shivered like one in the last throes of life. In his powerless hand he grasped a broken blade, which plainly told the history of his last short, but hasty combat.

"Look there, caitiff!" exclaimed the excited noble, pointing to the grave, "look there, where repose the bones of my father! See where his spirit stands in sorrow —his lustreless eyes gazing on thee, his murderer, and now on me, his avenger! Look at his hollow cheeks and bloodless lips! —made so by thee, villain; Lo where he stands, a dim and misty shadow of his former being, upon the roof of his obscure grave! See—his hand is raised—'tis the signal for mine avenging sword; Die, wretch! Go, and join thy fellow-assassins in the realms of the Infernal!"

Then dragging the body to the grave, he exclaimed—"Father! let thy troubled spirit rest: for here on the altar of thy grave, I immolate thy murderer."

The sword of the frienzed noble passed thrice through the breast of the usurer, and the dreaded President of the Tribunal was no more.

CHAPTER X.

THE ROBBERY AND DISCOVERY.

THE night following the incidents of the preceeding chapter, two fashionably dressed young men were conversing in a retired room of an hostel well known in Venice, at the time of our tale, as the "Inn of the Golden Grape." It stood on the broad quay Orfano, and was the favourite resort of the young nobles and higher ranks, as its wines, edibles, smoking-reeds, and accommodations were said to be superior to those of any other hostel in Italy.

A round table was before them, on which two large waxen tapers burned, throwing a bright light on the spangled and jewelled gear of the gallants, as they quaffed their goblets of generous grape, during their whispered speech.

"I tell thee, Leon, no harm can possibly come of it; we proceed with despatch and secrecy," said the taller of the two, in a low, cautious voice, and draining his cup of its mellowy juice.

"But we need more help," responded his companion, half falteringly : "if we should be surprised——"

"We need not be surprised," persisted the former, earnestly ; "if we but take the proper hour, and use sufficient precaution, neither noise nor scuffle shall ensue. What need, then, of other confederates, to whom we must allow an equal share of the spoil? Besides, how know we that they would keep their own counsel, after the deed? They might betray us, and then shame and ruin would be our portion. No—no! we must have no more sharers in that rich booty There will be none too much—even though there should be a thousand times more than I suspect—in his strong box. Besides think of the girl—for, despite what I have said, I do not believe she is yet wedded to the old man—is there not joy, rapture, more than bliss in that thought? Speak, shall we hazard it?"

"I care not if we do," replied the other, slowly, "provided thou art certain there is no danger in the attempt, and that, after the usurer is dead, thou wilt share fairly in the monies and jewels."

"I pledge myself to as much. Is it a bargain?"

"It is." replied his companion, giving him his hand.

At this moment, the door of the chamber opened, and a young fashionable presented himself to the eyes of the plotters.

"Ha! Lorenzo, my gay madcap," exclaimed the first speaker, his sober countenance changing, all at once, to the roysterer's careless smile, "I give thee good even! What circumstance indebts us for thy most welcome company!"

"Have ye heard the news?" said the new comer, 'seating himself, and clearing his throat with a draught of the tempting juice before him.

"In good sooth! not I," replied the roue, "I, for one, am no newsmonger. But to what do you allude?"

"The usurer—the life of the money-mart—has not been seen 'on change' to-day."

"Indeed! The reason?"

"I have not heard. Some suppose him ill—others, that he is engaged in forming a contract with the devil how to get all the currency of Venice in his grasp. I confess that I incline to the latter opinion myself."

"Ha! ha!" laughed the roue, glancing meaningly at Leon, "doubtless, it is so: for the white-haired knave hath either had his soul so deeply wrapt in the study and worship of Mammon, that it is no wonder if he hath now, in his old age, sacrificed a day in studying out how to change his copper into gold. Why, my merry hearts," he continued, re-filling his cup, and emptying it at a swallow, as if to quiet the restlessness which had seized upon his nerves by the intelligence brought by Lorenzo, "do ye not recollect how, some ten or twelve years agone the old wretch was absent from the mart two whole days ; that, when he returned, how desperatelely he plunged into the stocks, outbidding all, till it seemed as if he meant to buy up all Venice? Do you not remember it?"

"I was young then," said Lorenzo; "but I remember the sensation it made throughout the city."

"I have a recollection of it, too," added Leon; "it was about the time of the mysterious disapperance of the elder Galliano."

"Exactly," said the roue, his cheek changing colour, "it was the very time. And, my life on't! this is but another of his tricks ; and, it will be well for our impoverished merchants, if his re-appearance to-morrow, or next day, be not followed by the same disastrous result."

As he spoke, his eyes met Lorenzo's ; a sickly smile hovered round the lips of the latter.

"But come, my merry hearts," cried the roue, "let us forth. The night is tempting, and woos us forth. I would not stay in-doors on such a night for the brightest smile of my mistress. Come!"

"Nay, I prefer the grape and weed," said Lorenzo, filling his cup to the brim. Soon as this goblet is emptied, and this sweet-flavoured Turkish powder was

in clouds, I shall hie me home : for I have a chiding letter to write to my fair
mistress, ere I seek slumber ; and I must drink wine enough to nerve me for
the task."

"Chide her not too harshly," said the roue, laughing, and leaving the room, followed by Leon.

They passed through the hostel, laughing, and nodding carelessly to those whom
they met.

They walked on, in silence, each busy with his thoughts, till they reached an
unfrequented part of the quay.

"Hold'st thou still thy mind ?" said Leon, breaking the silence.

"Listen, and then judge," replied the other, with great coolness. "For the
last eight months I have run out, in extravagance, upwards of four thousand
No. 6.

ducats; a thousand of which was furnished me by my father. The rest was ob
tained partly from the usurer, and partly from friends who must be paid. Most of
the money falls due within a week, or my credit is lost. The notes held against
me by the usurer I care not a straw for, as I do not mean to pay them; and he
dare not seize upon me, partly because I am son to the first man of Venice, and
partly because he is aware of a secret of his in my possession, which might harm
him, if revealed. But I am in direst need—creditors—impertinent varlets!—dog
my heels at every step—my father's patience and kindness are exhausted, and I
must have means to hold my head up, as beseems my birth. The mammon-eaten
bags of the old usurer can supply my wants, and—they shall!"

His face was pale, but not with fear; his lips were bloodless, but not with
morse; his eyes were cold and stony, but not with shame. A haughty smile
hovered round his lip, and a slight blue shade was visible under his eye. His whole
aspect was terrible.

His companion, who, so far as his means and prospects were concerned, was
scarcely a jot better off, surveyed him, a moment, with awe. But as his nature
was not above temptation—as he loved pleasure, and cared but little for honesty,
when she interfered with his dearer mistress, pleasure,—as, moreover, he had been
for years, the boon companion and co-mate of Leonardo Foscari, in all his scenes
of dissipation,—his awe soon gave way to impatience, and he flattered the bent
of the young lord by exclaiming—"Time wanes; let us on!"

"So be it!" replied Foscari, laconically.

They passed on.

A few minutes of travel brought them to the street in which the usurer's house
was situated. Everything seemed to favor their purpose. The street was silent
and, apparently, deserted. The moonbeams shone on the side opposite the house
they were about to enter, and the house itself was shaded. Were not their prospects bright?

They neared the door, and paused. Were they conscience-stricken?

Lo! they are masked. And now they press against the door, gently at first—
anon, heavily. In vain: it yields not. A thought strikes the noble—he whispers
to his companion, and they leave the door. The house beside the usurer's is old,
tenantless, and ruinous. They press against its door—it yields, and now, they
are in darkness.

Hark! voices are heard—low, confused, but still voices, aye, and human as
their own. The sound of pickaxe and spade as they clash against each other, or
strike into the earth, is heard. A faint gleam, like unto that of the solitary star
sometimes seen in the heavily-curtained sky, at night, stole through a crevice in
the floor. Foscari bent over the spot, and, with his dirk, widened the crevice.
The sounds now were plainer, but naught was visible, save the torch-gleam.

Foscari groped round the floor cautiously. Joy! his fingers touch an iron ring.
A trap-door is in his grasp—'tis raised—and now—!

His eyes fall on a tableau that turns his naturally strong nerves into wavering
reeds.

In was a strange and startling picture. The vault was lit by a huge, flaming
torch, which, resting in the earth, near a pile of fresh dug earth, threw a broad
brilliant glare around the terrific scene. Standing in a grave, and holding in his
hand a fleshless skull, stood a masked figure, in the guise of a gondolier. A few
feet from him, his left hand resting on the edge of a new made and open coffin,
which was mounted on a pair of cross-legged stools, stood another in the same
garb and masked. Behind the latter, and near the coffin's foot, stood a tall, majestic personage, enveloped in a mask and cloak, and wearing a low-crowned circular cap, surmounted by a cluster of raven plumes; while, at the side of the
grave, his left hand holding a white waxen taper, and his left a long, slender cross
stood a monk, also masked and cloaked. As the skull was raised by the figure in
the grave, the form of the capped figure was seen to tremble and turn away, as if

shaken by some internal agony—but no word no sigh, no groan escaped him ; his grief was not for other's eyes.

The grave-digger, after a moment's survey of the skull, handed it, silently, to the figure on his right, by whom it was laid silently into the coffin.

Plying again his pickaxe and spade, the figure in the grave soon drew forth a few half decayed bones, which were also placed in silence, in the coffin.

"They are all there," said the figure, now leaping out of the chasm, and with the other counting the relics of the dead.

"They are," added he to whom the bones had been handed, arranging them in the shroud.

"Then, children," said the monk, advancing, "let us to prayer."

On the bare earth they knelt, that little and solemn group ; their caps off, and their heads bent, and their hands clasped in holy and heart-feeling prayer.

The holy words were o'er ; all rose, but that lone form whose heart was bent the most ; whose cheek was palest, whose eyes most dim with tears—the loftiest, the bravest, the proudest, the noblest of them all.—From his pocket the monk drew forth a phial, containing holy water, and sprinkled the relics. Then opening his missal, read the prayers of his church for the dead ; which, being done, the water was again sprinkled over the bones. The ceremonies being concluded, the most thrilling one to the noble youth at the foot of the coffin, now presented itself ; it was the closing and screwing of the coffin lid. During its operation, he rose from his knees, and leaning against an upright beam, near the staircase, gave vent to his o'ercharged heart, in a stream of mournful tears.

The lid was closed—the last screw rivetted into the wood —when one of the figures drew from a sack, a black velvet pall, and threw it over the coffin.

The noble resumed his stern bearing—the gondoliers raised the bier upon their shoulders—the monk seized the torch from its niche in the earth, and thus, the noble leading in silent procession, they ascended the staircase, and the vault was in darkness.

The hall was reached—the door opened, and, slowly and solemnly, the party marched forth. A few stragglers, fresh from scenes of mirth and vice, were passing up the pave, singing snatches of low, lewd songs ; but their mirth was checked by the strange and sudden sight. On beholding the priest, as he marched in the rear, with cross in one hand and the flaming torch in the other, their voices were hushed, and doffing their caps, bent their heads till the procession was passed and beyond their sight.

The moonbeams shone on the jetty pall, as it was borne to the quay Mazolio, a few yards from the usurer's house, and the stars looked bright as it was placed carefully in the gondola, which was to bear it to the ancestral vault of the Galliano family.

The noble seated himself sternly at the helm—the bier rested lengthwise, on a bench, brought for the purpose, in the centre of the boat—the monk took his station forward—the gondoliers taking their seats near the stern, raised their oars, and the next moment the little barge was gliding rapidly over the smooth waters, in the direction of a little island, where stood a mansion, towering above the rest, known as the home of the Gallianos.

Return we, now, to the watchers.

Foscari understood at once the meaning of the ceremonies attendant on the disinterment, and in the form of the masked stranger recognised the favourite of the metropolis, and his once beloved friend. His companion was not so fortunate in comprehending the scene, but Foscari enabled him to gather enough to form a dim conception of its meaning, by pretended conjectures and exclamations.

The darkness was no obstacle to Foscari, for he well knew, by repeated visits to the house, where to find appliances to furnish him a light, and, leaping down into the vault, groped his way to the staircase. Ascending, and searching an apartment in the rear of the house, he found box, flint and tinder, by which he as soon in possession of a light. A portable lamp, with three small burners stood on a mantle before him, and touching the igniting wick, he was soon in pos session of light enough to guide him back to the vault.

"Thou may'st spring," he exclaimed, to his companion, and holding the lamp under the trap.

Leon leaped down, and for the first time, the hopeful youths had a full view of the objects around them. In one corner, cold and stiff, and gory, lay the body of the usurer; his glassy eyes staring full upon them; while at the foot of the stair-case, as if he had fallen headlong from the top, lay the corpse of the gigantic black—its features betraying the last agonies of death. The youths started at the sight, and Foscari exclaimed,—

"By St. Peter! there has been foul murder here. It would be well to inform the authorities of the matter; what thinkest thou of it?"

"We had better see if his money bags have been jilted of life also," answered Leon, nervously.

"Right, business first—pleasure afterwards," responded Foscari, laughing. "Let us examine yonder arch, perhaps, as the doors are fast, they have neglected to add theft to their crime."

They proceeded to the first of the arches, but were somewhat staggered on finding no means of opening it, as the lock was on the inside. They then advanced to the next, and to the next, but the same unpleasant sight greeted them at each.

"Where, in Satan's name, is the master-key of these treasure caves," said Foscari, impetuously, and glancing uneasily around.

"The girdle of the black," said Leon suggestively.

"Psha!" exclaimed the other, contemptuously, "think'st thou the cunning gray-beard silly enough to trust the magic key of his whole wealth to that foul carcase?" More likely his own breast."

"Then, try, thou that," responded Leon, "while I examine the mute."

"So be it," said Foscari, hastily, and advancing towards the corse of the usurer.

"'Tis not here," said he impatiently.

"But 'tis here," cried Leon, joyfully, holding up a bunch of cunningly-devised keys, which he cut from the leathern girdle of the mute.

After several attempts, Foscari succeeded at last, in hitting on the right key, and in opening the first arch. But, nothing but shelves of parchment met their gaze. Giving vent to his disappointment in an oath, the roue proceeded to open the next, but with no better success. The third and fourth arches were opened, and found to contain little packages, evidently pledges, of rings, and jewels of considerable amount.

"Cospetto!" exclaimed Foscari, "but the knaves have left us something, after all. Here," and he handed handful, after handful to his companion, after having filled his own pockets first. "But the gold itself," he added, impatiently, "I must have that. This trash may do for those who want it."

He did not, however, disencumber himself of what he had already in his pos session.

The fifth arch was opened, and then what a sight greeted his gaping eyes. On broad shelves, extending from side to side of the arch, lay heaped piles of glittering coin.

"Ho, ho! my merry heart." he exclaimed rapturously, to his companion, who was busily engaged in helping himself to the little packages in the next cell, what thinkest thou of this? Is it not a feast to the hungry. Look."

But he gave Leon little chance for sight, he commenced filling his own pockets with the tempting food.

Leon exerted his utmost to grasp the golden coin, but so violently did Foscari repulse him, so eagerly did the roue seek to clutch it all, that he had but a small prospect of reaching any without a struggle. Desperate at the rapacity of his companion, and eager to seize upon a pile of ducats on the third shelf, he violently thrust the hand of Foscari aside, and, in the struggle, the stirred shelf gave way, and down tumbled coin, shelf and all upon their heads.

A bag of gold of considerable weight, concealed behind some piles of ducats, fel with them, and with such force that, striking the young lord on the breast in its descent, it felled him to the earth, where he was soon covered with the coin swept from the shelves by Foscari. When the greediness and rapacity of the latter had somewhat abated, he exclaimed,—

" Now, Leon, take thy share, and let us be gone."

But Leon answered not.

" Leon !" he exclaimed, looking around, " Leon, where art thou ? '

No answer came.

Springing over the heap of treasure before him, his heel grazed something fleshy beneath him, and immediately after a sharp cry rang through the vault, and all was silent. Half suspecting the actual state of things, Foscari hastily flung the heap aside, and, to his horror, discovered a gash on the head of his companion, and his face and neck all covered with blood.

"Great Heavens !" he exclaimed, recoiling, "have I slain him ! Leon ! Leon !"

No voice responded to his own.

"Leon, 'tis I ; for Heaven's sake speak."

No answer came from the lips of the prostrate man. Foscari knelt, and placed his hand upon the heart of his friend—it was still.

Cold sweat rolled down the cheeks and limbs of the ro ie on this discovery, his knees trembled and his eyes grew moist. For a few mom nts, terror unnerved him and the finger of a child might have robbed him of his balance. Thought then came to his aid, and he was himself again. In that dark vault, where death reigned over three ghastly subjects—in that dark vault, where mammom yawned from his glittering cave—in that dark vault, with the life of earth before him—and three pictures of the king of terrors around him ; in that vault where fate seemed to level her shafts unerringly on all who entered it—in that vault of darkness and mammon, and death and terror, the strong heart of Leonardo Foscari did not desert him.

He seized the spade, and, like a ceaseless and fearless worker, threw up the earth, till a hole of sufficient size to suit his purpose was made, when he flung the body of his late companion in, and covered him with the soil. Having filled up the gap, and strewed the superfluous earth around, to hide the evidence of his crime, he shovelled the treasure back into the cell, yea, every coin, fastened each arch, and, with his pockets sinking with his ill-gotten gold, dep rted from the house.

As he closed the outer door, he beheld two muffled and masked figures on the opposite side of the street. But careless of, or indifferent to, aught in the shape of danger, he passed on, regardless of their presence.

" 'Tis my mine," he muttered, " from whose depths I shall, henceforth, draw mine income. The master-key of the cells is in my possession, the house door secret spring is known to me, and the entrance to the vault through the crazy cot known to me alone. A week must elapse ere the suspicions of the " Ten" are aroused, during which time, those arches must be emptied, and then, what care I how soon the bodies are discovered ? They are not my work. But for Leon, the fool, his greediness brought his doom upon himself, I had no hand in't. Ere a week expires the earth around his grave will have lost its freshness, and then who will suspect aught lies beneath other than common soil ? But if they do ? Wha then—I murdered him not, 'twas an ill-timed accident, no more. Psha, I am reasoning myself into an assassin. Ha ! ha ! ha !"

He laughed, but it was a faint laugh.

He journeyed home, and, as he sat beside his gay couch, he counted the gains of his crime. A smile played around his features.

Wine was within his reach—l.e drank, and the coin before him repaid him amply for his guilt,

Hiding the gold in his dressing-case, he wooed sleep.   But did it come?   Hath guilt a charter to refreshing, balmy slumber?

As the grey dawn first peeped through the lattice of his chamber, sleep threw her folds over his physical orbs.   But his mental vision—the conscience—slumbered that?

CHAPTER XI.

THE HOUSE OF MOURNING.

ERE yet the dial had told the hour of nine on the succeeding morn, the few domestics of the house of Galliano were assembled in the old reception hall, to witness the last sad rites of "holy church" over the ashes of the dead. The bier stood in the centre of the chamber, upon two mounted stools, around which on little circular tables, waxen tapers gleamed. A priest sat by the coffin, reading his breviary in silence, while the parties who were priviledged to attend the service, were gathering.

Two young females in deep mourning, sat together on a cushion of a muffled bench near the reverend man, while the few friends of the young lord of Galliano sat on muffled chairs in promiscuous groups around the bier. The young lord himself soon entered, attired in a suit of mourning, and took a seat at the foot of the bier.

He shed no tears, but his features bore those unmistakeable traces of true grief, which command more attention than even tears; and, as his large dark eyes fell sadly on the pall, every eye was moistened, every heart was touched in sympathy. There was a nobleness in his tearless eye, a majesty in his colourless cheek, yea, a solemnity on his pale, nervous brow which struck the assembled auditors with pity, and produced in each a willing readiness to die in his defence, if such sacrifice was necessary.   There was scarce a being in that chamber who had not, within the past few months, felt the blessings either of his courage or his purse; and there was not one but knew his love of right, his ardour as a patriot and a man, his nobleness of soul under every situation, and willingness to battle even for the most friendless in the hour of danger.   Yet in his grief—in that hour when he mourned over the new found relics of his murdered father—who could give him consolation?

His mother had long since taken her place amid the ashes of the kindred of her lord—he was motherless.

His father's bones now rested in their cerements—he was fatherless.

His only brother had sunk into the tomb in early youth, when the worm of that fell destroyer of the fair and beautiful—consumption—had eaten up his heart—he was brotherless.

His fair and angelic sister had pined and sickened, and died on the loss of her father—the young lord of Galliano was, in view of all the world, kinless.

Unknown to the Tribunal, he returned to Venice, and now, in his ancestral halls was sole heir to his ancestral name, and mourner over his father's dust!

The solemn rites of the holy church were now performed—and the remains of the noblest of Venetian nobles were borne, with measured step and solemn, into the family vault, and placed among the ashes of its kindred.

The rites were o'er; the guests returned to their homes, and the only pillar of the Galliano house retired to his chamber to glean that repose which the exciting incidents of the past three days had rendered doubly imperative.

CHAPTER XII.

THE HOUSE OF CONCEALMENT.

An humble dwelling, in a retired quarter of Venice, was Mastachio Benedetti's ; and a merry heart was Benedetti's; and a merry dame was Madame Benedetti; and a merry maid was Junetta, the daughter of these Benedettis.

Benedetti was a respectable citizen ; Madame Benedetti was a respectable woman, and a respectable citizen's wife ; and Junetta Benedetti, being the daughter of two such merry and respectable people, was, of course, a very merry and a very respectable girl herself. But it is a dangerous thing for the young of the sterner sex, when a young lady of respectable parentage has found such qualifications to recommend her as respectability, wealth, merry-heartedness and beauty, because such things are apt to engross their attention, rob them of their sternness, and render them love-sick: *i. e.* tender. When a youth is once touched with the disease commonly nicknamed love, he degenerates in dignity and manliness, until he becomes the veriest bondman imagination can picture. With his love a change comes over his mental and physical parts, which has every thing but dignity in it ; and it is not until he is either noosed or loosed, that he recovers his former manly nature. The fact is, while the love fever is on him, a man is a sort of pliant sapling ; and the object of his affections a sort of ladle, whose coquettry draws from him the greater part of the natural sap in his cranium. When he is knotted, he begins to get an insight of the real state of things around him. Romance is very deceptive ; and until matrimony sweeps it aside, man is a laughable and ridiculous animal. The gentle sex understand this fact intuitively, and, through life, man is their victim—their play-thing: in view of which facts, we wonder where man's charter is for predominancy.

These thoughs ran through the mind of Junetta, as she beheld, from day to day, how perfectly her beloved mother led her beloved husband round the matrimonial circle , and, as she fancied her mother's system of domestic government, she had made up her mind to run a cord through the nostrils of her beloved, whoever he might be, and lead him into obedience in the same masterly manner. But, somehow, or another, the youth whom, out of all her admirers, she esteemed the most, looked very like one who would stand but little of this kind of government. His features and general bearing bore the impress of one born to command, not those of one born to be led. At least, so Junetta thought, and she sighed as she pondered over it. Now, when a young maiden sighs over the result of thought, it is a pretty good evidence that she is diseased around the heart ; and that that disease is the result of too much thought upon the object that created it.

A young man, whose features proclaimed his recent entrance into manhood, knocked gently at the door of the Benedettis.

It was opened by a servant, and the youth, as if accustomed to the house, nodded familiarly to the servitor, and entered the sitting room without ceremony. When a youth is as far advanced as this, he is in a dangerous state indeed ; for he even forgets politeness.

"I am sure you might have knocked, Messer. Calvari," said Junetta, starting up in coquettish confusion, as though she had not seen him, through the curtained window, ere he knocked at the door.

"Indeed, my pretty lady," replied Messer Calvari, "so I might, if my head had not been so filled with thoughts of a certain young lady."

"To whom does Messer Calvari allude?" inquired Junetta earnestly, as though not aware, in the slightest of who that certain young lady could be.

He took her hand in his—he turned his eyes on her's—he twined his arms around her waist—he drew her close to his breast—he put his lips to her's—and he gave her to understand that way to whom he alluded.

Junetta appeared to be satisfied with the reply.

This introductory busines fineshed, Messer Calvari inquired if one Eugenia and a certain lady Isabel were visible.

Junetta pouted, as if jealous at the interrogatory.

"Nay, my beloved, I bear a message to them, from a gentleman in whose fate they are interested: and I have promised to use despatch," said the youth earnestly.

"But do tel! me what all this mystery means, Calvari," said Junetta, inquisitively, "I can't bear to live in suspense. Do tell me whó and what these strange ladies are, and who that strange man is that brought them here."

"Thou would'st not have thy Calvari forfeit his honor by a breach of faith, wou 'st thou, Junetta?" inquired the youth, earnestly.

"What, there is a mystery about them then? I knew there was, from the stange manner in which they were brought here by that Messer Galliano In the night he brought them—in the dead of the night—and I knew nothing o heir presence till I met them at breakfast. Father, nor mother, would tell me tany thing about them ; and, moreover, enjoined me not to speak a word about them in the presence of strangers, on any account. I declare its a shame ! so it is, that any modest and well behaved girl can't be admitted into a share of secret atters, as well as any one else !"

And the coquettish beauty appeared to be very indignant at her cruel treatment.

"And of course Junetta has not periled the safety of the unhappy ladies under her father's roof by disobeying her parents?" inquired the youth earnestly and tenderley taking her hand.

Junetta gazed fondly upon him, as she responded smiling,—

"Junetta loves her parents too much to permit any rash and idle curiosity of her's to bring them misery, or mar the happiness or safety of others. But," she continued in love's tone of tender reproach, "how comes it thou dost play the truant from thy Junetta so much of late ?"

"My studies——"

"Thy studies indeed ! As if they were so important to the world ! Ha ! ha ! ha ! You used to come and take me out on the lagoons every fair moonlight, and compare my eyes to the bright stars, my brow to the snowy clouds, my cheeks and lips to the blushing rose, and my hair to the locks of an elfin. But now if I see thee once a week, 'tis wonderful ; and even then, thou never comest, unless on some such message as to-night, to these fair and unhappy ladies. It is not fair. Besides, how dost thou know how thine absence may operate against thee, if thou persist in this unloving course? Are not our doors besieged, nightly, by brave and goodly formed gallants—and is it not possible that one of them—I need not say which—might steal away my heart without my knowing it? Stranger things than that have happened. Thy allegiance to thy lady love demands a constant attendance, and look that she exact it not !"

"Hast thou done, Junetta?"

"No, I have not done. Thou must pay me more attention, or I shall cut thee off from my favour."

"Must is a hard word, Junetta."

"I cannot help it. Oh, Calvari, if thou could'st but take in thy brain, the yearning that maid feels for the every visit of the man she loves ! If thou could'st but conceive her watchings on his expected presence – how her ear catches the slightest token of his approach—how her eyes traverse an hundred times an hour the path he is accustomed to approach her by—if thou could'st but comprehend her silent and ever-offered prayers for his present and eternal safety—the anguish of her he when he comes not—the joy delirious of her soul when she hears his footstep—then, then, Calvari, thou wouldst not wonder that she is anxious for his presence in lover's hours—night—then, then, Calvari, thou wouldst not marvel that she grows jealous when he plays the truant, or gives her slightest cause for believing he is indifferent to, or careless of her love."

Her speech was earnest, yea, and earnestly spoken, and its import and truthfulness struck deep into her lover's heart.

"Nay, but thou dost me wrong, Junetta," said he, kissing away the tears that danced upon her cheek ; "there's not a slave in Venice but has more holitime than thy Calvari. Sleep seldom greets these eyes for more than an hour at a time. I am struggling and toiling for a cause which shall yet bring joy and comfort to our isle. My poor brain is overtasked, and my erst strong limbs have lost their

No. 7.

iron, by my deep studies, severe toil, and broken rest. Thou dost not know, fair one, what it is to pass unnumbered hours, in thy solitary chamber, at a never-ending task; liable at any moment to be summoned from thy studies or thy bed, to give healing balm to the sick, or ease the pangs of the dying. Thou dost not know what it is to live in the eternal fear of such a dreaded power as the 'Ten,' in the following of such an art as mine; for learning is not paid with reverence or gold by our mysterious and terrible rulers; they regard the searcher after knowledge with suspicion, and once seized, what follows, but death. Thou dost not know what it is to struggle through the dark days and lonesome nights against poverty, with no other hope than that thy ceaseless efforts may, at last, be crowned with some small share of man's passport through life—success. If thou didst, thou wouldst not chide my unavoidable absence."

" Nay, I knew not before of the stern necessity of thy toil, or——"

" Nay, sweet one, apologies are needless. The day, I trust, is not far distant, when our old and gladsome evenings shall return; and then doubt not but that we shall be happy. But till then, if thy Calvari is tardy in his coming, be sure thy pangs at his absence are not more painful than his own."

" Wilt thou forgive me ?"

" By this kiss. Now lead me to the chamber of your fair prisoners: for what I have to deliver to them is of importance."

" Then tarry a moment, till I inform them of your arrival."

She soon returned, and bade the student follow her.

The back chamber on the second floor was closely curtained, and neatly furnished with white and red matting, three or four cushioned chairs, a picture of the virgin over the mantel, a guitar in one corner, a lute and a small circular table. The females were sitting beside each other, their arms around each other's waists, when our student entered. Junetta, after opening the door, immediately withdrew.

The student bowing, advanced and handed the Lady Isabel a small leaf of parchment, neatly folded, saying,—

" This, from the Messer Galliano to the Lady Isabel; and this, from the Messer Genaro, to his beloved, the fair Eugenia."

He gave an ivory cross to the orange girl. Isabel opened the note, it ran
" —

Beloved of my soul—these lines to thee, in haste, greeting:

" The hour when our country shall be freed from her oppressors rapidly approaches. After mature thought, I deem it better for thy safety and the well-being of the deeply-wronged Eugenia, that ye prepare to leave your present abode and take shelter in the dwelling of a friend whom I have made in the isle of Cyprus. There, till the storm be o'er, and our oppressors swept away, thou canst remain in safety. I would have sent this warning to thee last night, but circumstances, of which I will hereafter inform thee, prevented my so doing. Be in readiness by the midnight of to-morrow, when I, with a couple of trusty friends, shall be with thee.

" Thine through time and eternity,

" GALLIANO."

When she had concluded her perusal of the note, Isabel took a ring from her finger, and, handing it to the student, said,—

" This to the gentleman who sent thee—say that that circle represents the un-broken faith the unfortunate Isabel has in his honour, and that I shall be prepared at the hour he names."

" I shall so report, honoured lady," said the student, bowing.

" Hast thou no answer for thy beloved ?" asked Isabel of her companion.

" The orange girl's lip quivered, and her cheeks coloured, as she replied,—

" The hour is past when I could speak of love; the hour is fled when I could return truth for truth, or plighted faith for plighted faith; I fear I must return his token !"

" And break his heart !" exclaimed Isabel, staying her hand as she was returning the white cross to the student.

The latter, though well acquainted with Eugenia's history, was too much of a novice in the study of woman, not to be surprised at this movement on her part, but he had the presence of mind enough to conceal its effect upon him.

Eugenia, bursting into tears, exclaimed,—

" What should I do, lady ?"

" Give him a token," replied Isabel, smiling, " but send not back his own. Thy ring for instance, or something that thou dost prize, and so prove thy willingness to make a sacrifice for the returning of his good opinion."

Eugenia had a little golden cross around her neck, which she had worn since childhood. She gave it to the student, and, with an agitated voice, said,—

" Give him this—'tis all I have—but he will know how deeply I do prize it."

She wore it in her days of innocence, ere yet the brand of shame was emblazoned on her brow. It was the only relic of her happier days. Was it a wonder, then, she sighed on parting with it ?

" No word, no cheering sentence, to send with it ?" said the student, interrogatively.

" Tell him, Eugenia is grateful for his fidelity," replied the orange girl, in a tremulous voice, and with downcast eyes.

" A world is in that sentence," said the student, smiling respectfully. " Adieu !"

" Think'st thou he can love me ?" asked the poor girl, when they were alone. " Think'st thou—knowing as he does my shame—think's thou he can love me ?"

" If he be human, and aware of the vile arts by which Foscari first entrapped thy guiltless and too confiding heart,—if he is yet aware of thy sorrow, thy repentence, thy trials and thy persecutions—if he ever loved thee, I say, and his heart still be human, fear not but his re-proffered love is honest as his first."

" But, lady, if thy case were mine—if thou hadst been lured away from virtue's path as I have been—if thy soft heart had been ensnared and wronged, as mine has been—if, after the shame, thou hadst awoke to sense and misery,—if, knowing the nobleness of the heart you forsook, he, forgiving your great fault, should offer you again his hand and home and honoured name,—wouldst thou forget thine own sense of right, the world's sneer upon thy former shame, and his weakness in affiancing thee in thy shame—wouldst thou so outrage his name as to accept his new loyalty through thy short stay on earth ?'

Isabel pondered a while with a pale cheek and throbbing heart, as the timid eye of the orange girl rested on her ; then, without raising her eyes, replied, nervously,--

" No, so help me, Heaven! I would not!"

" I thought so—I knew so !" murmured the broken-hearted girl, sinking back in her seat.

That night was one of tears.

CHAPTER XII.

THE MEETING.

THE moon and stars shone brightly in the heavens ; the sky was like a blue arch, here and there dotted with specks of snowy clouds. The air, after a sultry day, was cool and refreshing to those within and without. The proclamation of nature seemed to have gone forth to all the children of earth—" Night reigns; cease your toil!" Nature seemed to invite the house-dwellers forth, that in the rich and beautiful combination of the beautious sky, the silver night orb, the bright and silent stars, the murmuring waters and the pellucid air, they might enjoy a foretaste of the Paradise of the holy.

A white-haired man, of the middle height, with a proud step and a noble mien, was pacing the marble pave in front of the ducal palace, and surveying the lofty pile of St. Mark's. His eye was large, dark, and bright ; his forehead was high, full and slightly wrinkled ; his nose was of the Roman mould, and his lip was small, and spoke much for its owner's firmness and decision; his chin was bold and pointed ; he wore a small moustache and beard, and they gave to his features a venerable and sage-like expression. He was cloaked, as much to hide his costume as to prevent the effects of the night air upon his person. This was Foscari, the Doge of Venice. It was his custom thus to traverse the pave, fronting his palace, on pleasant nights, and no particular object, other than the beauty and calmness of the evening, called him forth on the evening in question. But it was not his custom to turn his eyes so frequently and so earnestly on one spot during these short wanderings.

A strange form, cloaked and masked, and majestic as the pile itself, stood, in stern dignity, in the shade of the broad door of the entrance of the temple of St. Mark. A jetty cap, with a heavy cluster of plumes of the same colour, adorned his head. He stood there as motionless as a block of marble, contemplating, apparently, the motions of the duke.

Was he a spy ? The duke was hated by the " Ten "—feared for his impartial decisions in matter pertaining to justice, and his fearlessness in advocating and maintaining the rights of the poor against the insolence and tyranny of the rich and the noble—hated equally by the poor, because he spared no caste in his administration of the laws. Was the stranger a spy? If not, was he an assassin, awaiting the moment when the duke's back should be toward him, that he might plunge the cowardly steel, unseen, into the spine of his victim ? In either case, the duke had nothing to fear ; for his private guards stood on the steps of his palace, and within call at any moment, when he choose to summon them.

The moonlight was no favourer of murder, if that was the stranger's object.

The duke, to settle all uneasiness and gratify his curiosity, watched the moment, when the pave was clear of the throng passing to and fro the front of the palace, and walked slowly towards the door of the temple. The figure budged not at his approach.

" Who art thou ?" said the duke, when within a few paces of the stranger.

" A man," was the reply.

" Thy business here ?"

" To feed my humour !"

" Less pertness and more politeness would better become thyself and me. Whose knave art thou ?"

" Mine own."

" It would seem so, indeed, from the licence which thou givest thy tongue. What charter hast thou for standing in the portals of St. Mark's ?"

" Every true Venetian's."

" Ha ! thou usest strange language, Messer Braggart. Art thou mad, I pray ?"

" Not wholly ; though there be enough in our fair sea-kissed isle to change us all to madmen."

" I do not understand thee, knave."

" Then thy white hairs indicate more brains than their owner is master of ; for thou hast, at least, the semblance of wisdom. Fie upon thee, that thy years and experience have not taught thee yet to understand the prattlings of children, let alone the language and figures of men !"

" Knave, thou art pert !"

" Softly, good master ; thou didst first propound ere I did answer. If I have puzzled thee in my replies, thou shouldst have been content."

" Doth defeat teach contentment to the vanquished ?"

" Look at Venice, and judge for thyself."

" What shall I learn by looking ?"

"Much for the eye, but nothing for the tongue."

"Why not for the tongue?"

"Because we may see, but speak not."

"Give me light, I pray thee."

"It would be dangerous to my head."

"Nay, I am no babbler.'"

"Art sure?"

"Men call me honest; and honest men blab not that given to them in confidence. I think that I deserve my reputation."

"Men never know us truly. We know not even ourselves till we are tried."

"Do we even then?"

"Most veritably; we know then of what we are capable when tried by circumstance and interest. Hast thou been tried?"

"Oft."

"Deeply?"

"Deeply."

"By what gauge?"

"Truth—right—justice."

"And hast never found thyself a recreant to thy soul's interest."

"Never!"

"Old man—on the dome of this holy temple there is a cross guarded by angels, whose ears catch the lowest whisper of undefiled truth, and waft it up to heaven; they are truth's watchmen, and hover round the honest lip, like a halo of eternal light, as bulwarks against all evil; on the first syllable of falsehood, they, shrieking, fly away and never more return. If till now, thy tongue hath spoke no falsehood, on peril of thy soul, chase not thy angels from thee!"

"What meanest thou?"

"'Twixt thee and me there is a current of tell-tale air, which, as Venetian ether is dangerous to trust, might peril my safety, if my speech were in unison with my thoughts; if thou wilt step into this shade, or go with me where our converse can be free and dangerless, I will open my mind to thee."

"What if I object?"

"Thou canst, if 'tis thy humour; but if thou dost, the thing concerning which I would speak to thee will remain unsaid—perchance to thy sorrow and mine!"

"Strange man! there is a mystery in thy speech and bearing, which doth tell me there is a connecting tie between thy fate and mine. Follow me: and fear not."

The duke led the way, through a private door, and into the palace.

It was a pleasant room for converse they entered. It was the private chamber of the duke, and situated in the rear of the marble pile, and looked out upon the broad sheet of the moonlit Adriatic. The casements, of which there were five —were furnished in the most gorgeous style of the middle ages. The walls were hid by heavy arras of blue and crimson velvet; and on one side, the ducal bed stood prominent, ornamented with gold and azure: beside it, the easy chair in which the reverend noble sat and meditated when released from the cares and troubles of his office. A few feet from it was a small marble altar, whose top was garnished by a silver crucifix; in front of this, a low cushion, on which the old man knelt at morning, noon, and night, while offering up his prayers. A silver burner, rested on a toilet table of polished oak, between two windows. The floor was covered with a soft matting, ingeniously figured to represent the mosaic pave of a palace hall.

"Be seated," said the duke, on entering, and pointing to a high cushion near his favourite chair.

The mask obeyed.

"Now, to thy business," said the duke, seating himself. "To what doth it relate?'

"Thy son," replied the stranger, laconically.

"Indeed!—a new subject! Say on."

"He hath wronged a confiding heart—broken it—sundered it from all its ties and kindred—blasted its hopes and prospects—cut it off from all its earthly joys and the sunny days which, ere his presence blighted, promised a harvest."

"Her name?"

"Eugenia."

"Her rank?"

"Of the fourth caste."

'Has she kindred?"

"She had—his crime sundered her from them."

"Her age when wronged?"

"Sixteen."

"So, so! And this deed was committed——"

"Three years agone."

"Did he then desert her?"

"He did."

"And she since had led the life of——"

"A harlot? No, duke. She had still a soul when he, in sight of all the world, had made her honourless; and, when by him deserted, found friends."

"For her, and in her case, what wouldst thou have me do?"

"Justice."

"I am in the dark as to thy meaning."

"Compel him to render back the honest name he stole from her to gratify his lust."

"Art in thy senses?"

"I hold the wits given me by my God, and till he takes them from me shall deem me still as sane as e'er a breather this side the Eternities."

"What! the son of a Venetian doge wed a wanton?"

"No wanton, duke! but one, by his unmanly acts, torn ruthlessly from honor, and plunged into never-ceasing misery. The pangs are hers—the guilt, Leonardo Foscari's."

"But think of the shame he'd bring upon his ancestral name by such affiancement."

"I think of nothing but his guilt, duke. I am a Venetian born; and, from childhood up to the present hour, have reverenced Jacopo Foscari, the famed Doge of Venice, as the first and purest rule of any state on earth; have prayed for him, at early morn and dusky eve, as one beloved and renowned for his justice. I would not in my travels allow a taint upon his name to pass unvindicated or unpunished. I fought for him when a boy, and in his wars with the Turks have borne his royal banner through seas of blood and carnage; have ever loved him as a father; reverence him still, and would not let his glorious fame pass on to posterity blemished by his son. I would have him vindicate his fame and name when assailed by his dearest kin, as well as when attacked by those foreign to his eye and heart. I would have him ever just—to the lowly as to the noble—to the weak as to the strong—I would have him ever Foscari the just."

"But thou dost forget the ignominy such a marriage would bring upon our nobility—the danger to which our throne would be exposed from the indignant nobles of Venice by such an impolitic union!"

"Let the marriage be ever so secret, my lord duke, I care not, so long as it be done. The lease of life of the victim herself is fast drawing to a close; even if she live, she would not subject herself to the ridicule of the world by appearing as bride to the son of the great Doge of Venice. But she cannot live: for the worm, created by his hand, hath eaten up her heart—and she is nigh unto death. Do her sorrows justice, then, O duke; let her not die with the blight upon her name and soul for ever! Do it, and the prayers of her kindred, the prayers of her friends, yea, the prayers of the poor victim herself shall be recorded by thy name on the archangel's record when thy soul seeketh for entrance into heaven!"

The duke pondered.

"What if my son refuse?" he asked, after a pause.

"Thou art his father," was the meaning response.

"Thou dost not know him," said the doge with a sigh.

"He does not!" exclaimed a voice behind the arras.

The doge started, and coloured to the temples. The next moment, Leonardo Foscari stood before them.

"Thou hast overheard us, then?" said the duke angrily; "thou hast been playing the eaves-dropper. Shame on thee, son!"

"Nay, shame on thee, father," responded Leonardo, coolly, "who couldst give audience to the vituperation heaped upon thy son by yon vile slanderer!"

"'Tis well thou art in thy father's presence and 'neath thy father's roof," said the mask, sternly, "or thy base throat and degenerate heart should answer for thine insolence: as it is, I have no answer for thee other than scorn."

"Indeed!" exclaimed the other, mockingly, "then a time will come when we shall hold converse in terms more in consonance with our rank."

"Cease these idle threats," cried the duke, indignantly. "Go, my son—that I should call an eaves-dropper a son of mine!—go hence, till my conference is ended with this stranger. When he is gone, I shall summon thee, and look that thou be ready."

"But father—"

"Not a word, I charge thee. Go, and play not the spy again upon thy sire's privacy, or a doom thou little dreamest of, shall be visited upon thee."

Leonardo obeyed, with scowling brow, and wrathful step.

"Said I not thou didst not know my son?" said the duke, in a somewhat piqued tone.

"Thou saidst truly," rejoined the mask; "and I dare venture to assert your lordship hath never, till this hour, known how far his presumption could lead him from that manly path which honour hath ordained."

"I confess as much," returned the duke, testily; "and were it not for pity of his youth, I should have chastised his insolence on the spot. But enough of him; return we now to his victim."

"Which one, my lord?"

The duke glanced at the questioner—but the mask shrank not from his eye.

"Which one? Hath he wronged more that one?"

"That question, my lord, argues thy little knowledge of thy son. What would your highness think should I prove him a murderer and a thief, as well as a seducer?"

The duke turned pale and gasped.

"Saidst thou?—" he muttered, feebly.

"A spy, too, on his father's every word and act—a liar, and——"

The mask paused: for the duke had fainted.

The mask started back in confusion at his critical position, scarce knowing what to do. His eye fell on a small silver bell, standing on the altar. He rang it, and, a moment afterwards, a servant entered the apartment.

"Water, sirrah, in haste," cried the mask; "for lo! the doge hath fainted."

The servitor rushed out; as if he had heard the order—as if it had recalled him to consciousness, Foscari raised his eyes feebly, till they encountered his companion.

"Stay," he muttered, "what need of alarming the knaves for trifles? 'Twas but a slight touch of the weakness of age; but Heaven preserve me from them in future! Another such, and this beating pulse would soon be still. Tell me all—stay."

A host of servitors were now in the apartment.

"Beware, knaves!" he cried, angrily; "and wait till ye are summoned."

They departed in confusion.

"Tell me all," he repeated, addressing the mask; "tell me all, and spare not; thou seest how firmly I can bear it, now the first shock of amazement is over. Tell me all—all thou knowest."

"I have no more to tell," replied the mask; "I have given thee the outlines of his character : time will reveal to thee the minutiæ. Meanwhile, as the hour grows late, I'll take my leave. But ere I go, a word with your highness : on the night of the coming carnival, leave not thou the palace."

" And why not, mysterious man ? "

" Danger to thy person will then be avoided, your highness. More, I have neither the power nor the inclination to expose. But, as thou valuest thy life, pay heed to my warning."

" Explain thy meaning fully, strange man, or I shall summon and bid my servants to seize thee as one dangerous."

" Summon them," said the mask, coldly.

" Art thou so determined, so fearless in thy nature, then ? I implore thee to expound thy strange words."

" It would aid thee naught, and jeopardise myself," said the mask, with a stern laugh.

" Art thou my foe ?"

" Doth my conduct of to-night lead thee to so think, doge ?"

" Nay, I know not what to think : thy bearing is noble, thy voice manly, but thy conduct inexplicable."

" Time will unravel my mystery ; as neither force nor fair speech on thy part can enlighten thee now, take the wise man's alternative—time—and put thy faith in't !"

" Thou dost not hate me ?

" No, doge."

" Dost thou love thy country's chief ruler ?"

" With a patriot's love, ay."

"And thou dost know of a danger threatening his well-being, and yet concealest it from him ?"

" I have told thee enough to preserve thee from all danger, if thou but followest my counsel."

" What wrong in me, if I should now order thy arrest ?"

" What wrong, doge ? A foul wrong—a wrong that would blast thy fame through all time, and do thee not a jot of benefit—the base and treacherous wrong of inviting a stranger to thy house, and, taking advantage of thy power, robbing him of his chartered liberty. Durst thou do it, duke ? Thou durst not—it were too vile a deed for one so strictly just.'"

" Thou art right, strange man—I dare not."

" I know it—and, warning thee again not to quit thy palace on the night of the approaching carnival, I take my leave. Farewell !"

" A word, ere thou goest : Shall we meet again ?"

" We shall."

" Where ?"

" E'en there where circumstance shall place us."

" Ere long ?"

" Ere long, doge. Shall the wronged girl of whom I spoke be righted ?"

"If possible, ay."

" Without delay ?"

" As soon as I can prevail on my son to right the wrong."

" Wilt thou not compel him, doge ?"

" Thinkst thou he can be compelled ?"

" The man who, sheltered by small power, doth play the tyrant and the villain, can, by a power greater than his own, be compelled to aught—be it base or godlike ?"

" That is thy thought ?"

" 'Tis nature, doge."

" Thou hast studied that ?"

" All things befitting man to know that can be had for mental labour, know I."

" I fear me much, thou'rt but a braggart."

" Princes are privileged to doubt, and to speak their doubts."

"Thou art bold, too, as never a man in Venice is bold."

"He who would serve the cause of Truth must not enter her ranks with a timid heart."

"Thou art a courtier, by thy ready speech."

"Courtier I am not, your highness; but a plain, unpretending man. The airs of court agree not with my humour; at least those courts that I have seen. There is not enough of God's unpolluted essence sprinkled in their halls. I would not be a courtier, and am none."

"Thou art a strange, bold man."

"Your highness is at liberty to hold me in your thought as your inclination will; I have performed mine errand—warned thee and advised thee; and so, farewell!"

"Strange, strange man!" soliloquized the doge; "brave and honest, noble and proud, young and wise,—ah! why, why was I not blessed with a son like him!

No. 8.

But, for the victim of whom he spoke, yes, she shall be righted ! Leonardo must do her justice—lowly though she be ! It will teach him a lesson—perhaps incline him to wisdom. He is in that stage of manhood when sharp lessons have the most power in regulating and strengthening the mind. The lesson may make a man of him. He is wild, impetuous, frolicsome, half thoughtless ; and a bold act on my part might transform all his youthful follies into virtues. It shall be tried—my word is pledged, and justice must be done !"

He rang the bell—a servitor answered it.

"Go, and tell my son, his father awaits his presence."

The servitor bowed and withdrew.

"I'll have no refusal," soliloquized the doge, "he must consent to right his victim. I've borne his follies till they have ceased to be follies. I'll put up with them no longer. He hath a winning way with him, in excusing his errors ; but I'll be firm now, and insist on his giving them o'er for ever. If he braves me, I'll discard, nay, disinherit him. I'll be tender with him no longer."

Footsteps were heard in the hall, near the door.

"He comes, but not alone," muttered the doge ; "he fears my reproaches, and therefore comes in company. But I'll be stern and firm with him."

The door was thrown open rudely, and a huge black, cloaked and capped, and attended by six masked figures in black, entered the chamber.

The doge's heart sank, and his cheeks turned pale, and his nerves quivered and his voice trembled, as he demanded of the leader his business.

The latter, without a word, placed a sealed packet in his hand.

The doge broke the seal, and, with an effort, mastering his agitation, scanned its contents.

When its perusal was concluded, the statues fronting his ducal palace, were not more white than he.

His voice was subdued, his head bowed low to the dark bearer, as he responded —"I am ready—lead on !"

CHAPTER XIII.

THE EFFECTS OF THE ARREST.

Pass we now three days.

The faces of the nobility and citizens of Venice were marked with fear, mistrust, sadness. One might have read their thoughts in their eyes, without hearing a word from their ashy and quivering lips. As if an all-slaying plague were raging through the streets, the citizens kept in-doors, fearfully. The marts of trade were deserted, the shops closed, and the churches void of worshippers. Those whom stern necessity drove forth to traffic, did their business in laconic sentences, and downcast eyes, as if an universal edict had been issued, forbidding speech and action. Men met each other in the streets and squares, and, though their acquaintanceship and friendliness were unbroken, yet passed without a word or sign of recognition. A dark cloud seemed to hover over the fair city, although the sun shone glowingly, and the sky was lovely as ever. Doors were closed, windows heavily and closely curtained, as if the stricken ones within feared the eyes of the fear-stricken ones without.

One form alone was seen traversing the streets boldly. One form alone, amid the Fear-contagion dared to stalk through street and square, and look at the right and left, his large dark eye searching every face he met without a moment's quailing. Pale was his cheek, though ; pale his lip, as he read the Fear in the closed doors and curtained windows and hasty steps and downcast eyes, and caught the laconic and fear-choked words of those whose stomachs forced them into traffic,

Pale was he! but not with that paleness which marks the wretch whose timidity is caused by fear: but pale with that hue which the strong heart wears when indignation at man's cowardice takes the place of pity.

With hasty strides, his good sword hanging boldly at his side, he passed from street to street, from square to square, from quay to quay, from canal to canal, his eyes every moment searching each spot, before, behind and around him, as if in anxious pursuit of some loathed foe, or beloved friend.

So passed the day.

Night came; night, with all her beauties and magical influences; night, with her bright stars, sky drapery and moon, and soft, wooing air; night came, and one by one, as if ashamed of their cowardice, the inhabitants of Venice braved the outside of their doors. Still, the silvery laugh rang not in the air, and voices were not heard aloud, as in nights gone by. It appeared as if habit, not the loveliness of the night, brought them forth; and more like funeral followers they seemed, than beings forth for pleasure, so whispering they spoke.

On this night three men, guised as common gondoliers, met, as if by accident, at the foot of the quay Zechetti.

"Give thee good even, friend," said one, "art thou for a sail on the lagoon to-night?"

"Customers are scarce," replied the other; "I know not if I shall pull an oar, or pocket a piece of the mint."

"Nay, rather than pull not for reward, I'll e'en pull for mine own pleasure," said the third.

"I like thy spirit, friend," said the first, "and if thou hast no dislike to my company, will join thee at a tug."

"So be it, an' thou wilt," replied the other, "I've done nothing to-day, but sleep, and must have exercise. So jump in."

"Wilt thou not join us?" he added, addressing the remaining boatman.

"I care not an' I do," responded the other, leaping into the boat.

"Then take thy seat astern," said the owner of the gondola, arranging his oar, "for, till we are tired, thou can'st not exercise thy skill. Now, then, my merry hearts, let's dive into the breast of our ocean mother, and sing our passage out, in the merry strain of our craft. Hast thou thy pocket flute?"

"I have," responded the boatman at the helm.

"Then make the air ring with its tones," said the inquirer, "while we follow thee with our voices."

They pushed from the quay, and as they rowed forth, the flute led the strain, and the ears of those assembled on the quay, caught the following song:—

SONG OF THE GONDOLIER.

The night—the night—the night,
When the sky is calm and clear,
The night—the night—the night,
When the tide and shore are near.—

From the pier I leap,
In my boat on the deep;
And with bark all full,
To the lagoons I pull,
Cheerily! Cheerily!

The night—the night—the night,
When the sky is calm and clear;
The night—the night—the night,
When the tide and shore are near.—

From the crowded quay,
To the deep broad bay,
The lover with his love,
To my gondola move,
Cheerily! Cheerily!

The night—the night—the night,
When the sky is calm and clear;
The night—the night—the night,
When the tide and shore are near.——

Who will fly the quay,
And in my bark away—
Who will fly the pier
With the gondolier,
Cheerily! Cheerily!

The song died away in the distance; the persons congregated on the pier drinking the breeze of the sea, shrugged their shoulders at the temerity of the singers in disturbing !the silence of the night; and recollecting their own fears through the day, muttered to each other, as they glanced at the gondola, fast receding from the shore, "Bold fellows! bold fellows!" Many expressive "umphs!" and meaning glances were directed towards the boat also, as though the gondoliers had committed high treason by indulging in mirth. But example has a powerful effect, and our worthy cynics soon had sufficient courage to speak above a whisper, though their tones were not over loud at that.

Return we to the boat.

Soon as the gondola was far enough from the shore, to suit the purpose of the gondoliers, the owner of the boat exclaimed, in a low tone,—

"Enough of the song; it hath done its office, in blinding those on the pier as to our real purpose. Now to business. How speeds the cause?"

"Bravely," replied the second oarsman, "My men are ready—their knives are sharpened, their courage strong, their spirits buoyant, as the hour approaches."

"And thine, Gennaro?" said he of the stern, in a voice not to be mistaken, how much soe'er his garb might do him wrong.

"They wait the hour impatiently; each day but makes them more impatient. The days pass slowly."

"I thought so, to-day," exclaimed he of the stern, "as I passed from street to street, and beheld the cowardice of our inhabitants, in hiding within doors. Scarce a man to a street! and all because Foscari had disappeared so mysteriously. Is this the courage of our Venetians?"

"They have been used to terror for years," replied Gennaro; "rid them of the cause of that terror, and then see if their fears are greater than those of any other nation. The 'Ten' have held our speech and action in check so long—have robbed us of our rights and privileges for so many generations, that it is no wonder that at this their last and most daring deed, the people shrink aghast in terror. In fact, your lordship is not altogether free from the universal dread, else why that unseemly guise in which thou now art wrapt!"

"Not from fear have I donned it," responded the noble, "but from a fancy that it would save me from rude remark in my perambulations. I would see without being seen, and hold converse with the leaders of our cause without being noticed by vulgar eyes. But this aside—have ye no suspicion, after what I've told you of my conference with the duke, of the accuser's name?"

"Hast thou?"

"I have."

"Whom dost thou think?"

"Leonardo Foscari."

"What—his own son?"

"The same."

"Heavens! Can he be so lost to filial love and honour? The cause?"

"Nay, I suspect it only. But I opine that fear of his father's anger and reproaches led him to the deed. You know he is the leading spy of the 'Ten'—has, from that power, free license to do what he will against the laws, for his service as a spy upon those whom meaner spies cannot reach—and that he likewise receives reward for his unprincipled labours. Ye know all this?"

"We have so heard."

"My intelligence is beyond a doubt, and [subsequently confirmed by witnesses whose probity is beyond a peradventure. Ye must implicitly believe my reports, and speak of them, among our men, as facts beyond a doubt, else my labours in procuring them will prove of no avail. But to the main matter of this conference —how didst thou find thy sister ?"

"Ill in health—lowly in spirits," replied the second oarsman, whom the reader has ere this recognised.

"And the lady Isabel—thou saw'st her, also ?"

"Sad in spirit ; e'en as sad as my sister."

"Liked they their new abode ?"

"'Tis safer than their last."

"Sent they no message ?"

"Much the Lady Isabel blushed when your name was mentioned ; and much she trembled when I spoke of the sudden and mysterious disappearance of the doge."

"But no message?"

"None."

Galliano sighed, and for a few moments, gazed in silence toward the island where his beloved was concealed.

"All hope is o'er for thee, Isabel," he murmured, "if this our glorious cause succeed not; thy Galliano will not outlive his struggle for his country's freedom, and then, O Isabel! what, what will be thy fate. Kinless, harmless, poor and friendless, what, what will be thy fate ! But shall we fail ?—after all our secret meetings—our midnight watchings, our expenditure of time, and wealth, and blood,—our wrongs, our sufferings, and high hopes—shall we fail ? Great God forbid it !"

In good truth, the noble was sad at heart, yea, o'ershadowed to the very soul. The circumstances attendant on his father's death—the singular discovery of his father's grave—his burial in the old family vault—the scenes witnessed in the subterraneous dungeon—the sudden death of the father of his beloved—her own dependence, weakness, danger—his combat with and triumph over the black—his meeting with the usurer, and the latter's death over the grave of him he murdered—the doge's disappearance, perhaps death, and all through his means,—the gloom he witnessed o'er the city—all this floated through the chambers of his mind in images darker than the facts ;—was it then a wonder he was sad?

He thought of his own cheerless home—of the dark prospect before his beloved in case all his schemes for emancipation from the Tribunal's tyranny should fail —of the woe and ruin of all engaged in that great enterprise, if fortune, time and circumstance favoured not the cause—of the revolution in men and things, if the enterprise succeeded—of the blood that must flow, whether triumph or defeat was their guerdon for the peril—he thought of this, and he was sad,—very, very sad.

"Have ye any new proselytes ?" said the noble, in a deep voice.

"Seventy in our section, since our last meeting," replied Gennaro.

"And thirty-three in ours," added the other.

"Good !"

"When saw you last the secretary ?" asked Gennaro.

"An hour before dawn of to-day," replied the noble.

"What addition to his ledger since last report ?"

"Ninety."

"The work speeds on."

"Aye, bravely," said Galliano, in a more cheerful voice. "But as for the doge, he must not die. He is a friend to the people—opposed to the Tribunal—and loves freedom equal to the best of us ;—he must not die."

"How can we save him ?" said the gondoliers, anxiously.

"By hurrying on the hour when we strike for liberty," responded the noble.

"He is of too high rank for the Tribunal to hurry on his death," said Gennaro. "We had better look to the cause first ;—the hour rapidly approaches—to hasten it were dangerous."

"Thou dost not know the 'Ten' for all that thou hast suffered," said the noble ; "'tis the Tribunal's policy, once their victims are in their power, to hurry on their doom. It lacks but a week of the Carnival, and, ere that time, the chances are an hundred to one that the mock trial, sentence and death of the doge will be over. In which case, what new tyrant will be planted on the ducal throne ! It were best to strike at once, and, saving ourselves, preserve the duke."

"It were dangerous," said Gennaro, "for any cause soever, to change the day or hour for striking ; our preparations are made for the Carnival night—our men have been told to look forward to that night for the signal—their minds have no other thought. To change the time, or for an earlier hour or later, would change their thoughts, mar their plans, and perhaps chill their patriotism. Knowing the minds of the rude ones in our section, I think a change would be dangerous to thy cause."

"Well, we'll let it pass," said Galliano, gloomily. "Row in ; perhaps fortune may save the old man without our aid. I shall not see ye again till the last meeting night, when, if fortune fail me not, I shall bring ye a proselyte ye little dream of. Row in."

The gondola was turned towards the shore ; and, as it flew over the waters, a huge crowd was seen congregating on the pier from whence our heroes started.

"Something is going on there," said the noble, in an excited tone. "I know not what it is, but my heart misgives me ! On your lives, row in !"

The gondoliers needed but little bidding ; for that natural fear which creeps over men when conscious that those they love may be in jeopardy, lent fiery strength to their arms and sped their bark with the speed of lightning to the pier.

The noble sprang hastily from the boat, and made his way through the crowd ; and, when his companions had neared the spot on which he stood, they beheld him standing in triumph over the prostrate figure of one well known to, and loathed by, every son of Venice—Leonardo Foscari !

"Coward ! dastard !" exclaimed the excited noble, waving aloft the sword he had wrenched from the prostrate roue, "are acts like these the charters for thy manhood ? Hast thou neither soul, nor honour, nor shame left in thy foul, filthy carcase, but thou must play the dog for ever ? What ! steal women from their homes by night, when their defenders are away and beyond their cries ! Take that, cowardly slave !" and as he spoke, the foot of the excited and indignant noble was plunged into the side of the wretch : "take that !" he added, "and bear it as living mark of thy unworthiness to be punished by the sword !"

The miserable wretch groaned at the pain inflicted upon his person, and gasped with a demon's passion. Starting up, he ran up the pier with wild and hurried speed, and uttering threats of vengeance.

All gave way fearfully before him, and many of the crowd, fearing lest spying eyes should be upon them, stole from the spot noiselessly, and soon were lost from view. Ere those who remained had time to recover from the sudden and startling incidents, the young noble, his companions and two young female forms were seen in the gondola, and rowing fast from the shore.

The forms on the pier, as if aware of the danger of being found there after such a scene, were soon scattered over other parts of the city, and the quay was deserted, all wondering when Venice would be like the Venice of olden time, free from broil and tyranny and wrong.

CHAPTER XIV.

THE EXPLANATION.

THE boat swept over the water like a bird fleeting from the deadly gun of the sportsman. A little island, containing about an hundred houses, was the spot on which the boat of the gondola was directed. Having reached a broad stair flight, the rescued females were hastily landed, and escorted by the noble, borne to an obscure looking dwelling on the eastern part of the isle. The gondoliers, immediately afterwards, released their bark, and, again plying their oars, pulled for an island about three hundred yards distant ; on reaching which, they pulled their boat ashore, and, covering it with a quantity of old canvass, thus giving it the appearance of a boat which had lain there for some days—fled, hastily, to a low-looking shed about forty paces distant from the shore. They were met at the door by one of their own caste and costume, to whom they hurriedly related the cause of their sudden appearance, and with whom they immediately departed to another dwelling, of the same rude caste, in another part of the island.

Return we now to the rescuer and the rescued.

When they had reached the dwelling, the noble conducted the females into a neatly furnished apartment on the second floor, where, after pointing out to them a secret door, and discovering to them the manner of its opening, in case of a surprise, he left them, saying he would soon return.

Descending the staircase, the noble entered the front apartment, where he was met by a middle-aged man, whose costume at once proclaimed his calling.

"Oh, good master goldsmith," said the noble, smiling, "I have used the privilege thou gavest me—and, lo! thy chambers are in my possession. Two fair beings, whose misfortunes and persecutions are only equalled by their beauty, are now in thy charge."

"Aught in my humble power to serve them, shall be heartily given, my lord," replied the goldsmith.

"At another time, my good friend, I will tell thee of the cause of my sudden appearance here, and of the wherefore of my guardianship of the ladies who now lodge beneath thy honest roof."

"It matters not, my lord," replied the goldsmith ; "that they are under your protection is sufficient for me that they are ladies of worth. How speeds the cause ?"

"Bravely ! our next meeting will make the most sanguine of us leap for rapture. Meanwhile, thy lady will do me honour and great service by keeping close the fact of her knowledge of our fair unfortunates."

"I pledge myself for her secrecy, my noble lord."

"Enough, my honest friend. As time is precious, and as my fair friends may need my presence for a few minutes, I'll take my leave."

The noble hurried up stairs.

Isabel and Eugenia were in tears, by the window, as he entered.

"What ! weeping, fair ones !" he exclaimed, taking a seat near them. "Shall the villain have it to boast that he can make us all weep, whene'er he lists ? Nay, cease, as ye love me ! I ne'er could bide the sight of tears—they rob me of my manhood, and turn me back, in years and feeling, to a weak and timid child."

"Have we not cause for weeping ?" said Isabel.

"Nay, I'm no woman and cannot answer thee," said Galliano, with a smile. "Men think not of weeping o'er a wrong—they redress it straight, and, in the joy o'er revenge, laugh till all remembrance of the deed is swept away. But tell me, lady, how it chanced I found ye so far from that asylum in which I placed you. Methought my measures for preserving you from all further persecution by Foscari were most effective."

The orange girl blushed, and exclaimed,—

"The fault was mine, my lord, and on me let your anger fall."

"Nay, fair trembler, responded the noble, "your severe sufferings swallow up all anger. Give me to know how it all has chanced, that I may take warning and prevent the further visits of the princely libertine."

"The night was fair," said Isabel, "and, weary of our room, we sought the garden. A small arbour invited us, where, as we inhaled the evening ether, we spoke of our several destinies, our past, our present, and our future. While speaking thus, a strain of music, proceeding from the garden next our own, fell upon our ears. We paused to listen; anon, arose, and approaching the fence, drank in the sounds of the melodious instrument, till our souls forgot their woes, and were wrapt in bliss. Thus we stood, entranced, when he, Foscari, suddenly stood before us. Palsied, by fear, we scarce could speak; and when our tongues had found free utterance, we were being dragged from our house of refuge to the beach. We screamed and struggled, but none came to our aid, for the villain had a band of fierce and armed knaves around him, whose bright swords awed the few that we encountered on our way. Brought to the beach, we were hurried into a boat filled with stalwart and masked rowers, whose stout arms soon bore us far from shore. The wretches gagged us to silence our screams, while he, the chief villain, held our arms, and with insulting words bade us struggle not, or we should be plunged into the deep. We were silent, unresisting, till we were landed. A crowd was gathered round the pier; and in the hope that some brave heart would attempt our rescue, we screamed and struggled as they bore us up the pier. Nor were we mistaken; for our young friend, Calvari, was among the crowd, who, recognising our voices, and divining the rank and intentions of our abductors rushed boldly forward and felled the foremost wretch, who held us to the earth. The rest catching the spirit of his courage and enthusiasm, rallied to our defence. Foscari at length declared his name and rank, and bade them stand back on peril of their lives. They all gave way but Calvari, who, fearless of everything but our danger, seized me and bade the villains do their worst. The wretches paused, fearing lest the crowd should fall on them again; when Foscari rushing forward and dealing him a blow, commanded his myrmidons to seize and bear us to the palace. They hesitated, and he, to inspire them, seized us, and bidding the crowd give way, was dragging us onward, when your timely arrival saved us from further outrage, and punished the foul dastard."

"Enough! enough!" said the noble, gaily; "yea, more than enough," he muttered to himself, "I thought him base before, but knew not till now the perfection of his villainy. But the hour is coming for him, and for all his kind. Till then, we'll let him pass. Ye are safe here," he continued aloud, and rising; "the suddenness of our flight and this change in your abode will baffle the vigilance of the keen villain. A few days and all shall be quiet, all at rest. Our friend, the goldsmith, and his kind dame, will be your guardians in my absence. Everything necessary to your well-being will be by them provided. I need not warn you of being careful to preserve your faces from strangers, nor of listening to music in neighbouring yards," he added, smiling. "There are other cavaliers as dangerous as the gay Foscari. And now," he took their hands, and his voice faltered as he spoke, "farewell! for five days you must not expect to be visited by the gloomy Galliano. Duties weighty and imperious will detain me from paying my respects to all save a few stern friends, and they reside not in this isle. Farewell, Isabel; farewell, Eugenia, brighter days I trust are in store for us. The clouds are not always dark, and the sun is not always hid. But when I come to ye again, I shall look for the smiles that adorn beauty and spur men on to high and glorious deeds! Another shall accompany me,"—he glanced at the blushing orange girl—"whose presence, I trow, will add more joy to thy heart than thou hast felt this many a day. Farewell, again—and may he who watcheth o'er the shelterless lamb as o'er the housed one, protect ye till my return!"

The orange girl sank back with emotion.

The Lady Isabel accompanied the noble to the door, her hand still lingering in his.

Galliano trembled, as he felt the pressure of that soft hand. It sent a chill through his stern frame that robbed him of his collectedness. At last unable longer to withstand the force of his passion, he clasped the peerless, unresisting beauty to his breast, and, in one wild, long, burning kiss, told at once his long concealed and ardent love.

No. 9

CHAPTER XV.

THE LAST MEETING OF THE CONSPIRATORS.

It was the night before the carnival.

In a vault of some two hundred and eighty feet in length and about one hundred and twenty in breadth, were assembled a host (for they were countless) of masks. Skull caps adorned their heads, hiding the dark and grey locks of every member of the assemblage. A host, we say, a host of masked heads. Their forms were dominoed, so that it was impossible to catch the slightest sight of the gear they wore. Like one massive body of human forms conjoined they seemed, as they stood in close proximity to each other from wall to wall of the long, broad vault. A sea of human heads, silent and breathless as that assembly of old which waited the moment of the tyrant's entrance into the imperial hall of the capitoline city that each " might kill his share of him."

Silent were they, as if on each one's speechlessness depended the lives of the united throng. In one direction their eyes were turned, and there, on a rough and temporary stage, an altar stood ; a lamp, with five burners, suspended from the ceiling, threw a bright glare on the open leaves of a written volume, whose characters symbolic, together with a bare dagger, a skull on each side of the books, struck awe into every heart of that mighty throng. Grim and gaunt and terriffic, yea, and majestic was that altar. In gazing on't, and on its eloquent symbols, a thrill ran through the multitude, enthusiastic as that of the pious pilgrim who has spent months in weary travel to his favourite shrine.

On one side of the altar, and in view of the whole assemblage, sat a masked figure, with a large volume before him, over whose pages he appeared to be absorbed in patriotic earnestness. Like the rest of the assembly, he wore a domino, which enveloped him from head to foot. The excitement was high, as was evinced by the quick breathings which, like the first swell of ocean, ever and anon, rose up and fell back into the bosom of the throng.

Why was that multitude so silent? Feared they speech would betray them, if they dared to use it? Or, tarried they a leader to open their proceedings? The hour is late, and yet, though the assembly is huge beyond conception, no word hath been spoken, no form of meeting opened.

Hark! a sound as of a muffled gong! lo! the assemblage breathe freer—that sound, what doth it betoken?

Lo! the front of the altar sinks, and within two forms are seen. Their rank is noble, or else nature hath made men wear the aspect of nobility, without the silken charter given by man to man to proclaim him above the common herd. Hark to that shout, deafening as the sudden peal which the dark and angry clouds roll forth, when the elements would fling the fear pall over the hearts of the Triune's images. Again the peal rings forth as if to split the earth above into countless fragments. And now, lo! a masked but gallant form enters from the altar's bosom leading a weak and tremulous companion into the presence of the mighty throng. The face of the latter is bare, and on his reverend brow and cheeks a tale of recent and terrible agony is written, as if the veil which hides the caves of the Infernal King from human vision had been opened to him alone of all the breathers this side the abyss of eternities. The shout of the multitude ceases on his appearance, and mouths are agape with wonder. Murmurs run through the vault, and whispers of half-believed treachery are audible. Concealed knives are half-drawn from their sheaths, and half-suppressed mutterings tell the danger of the new comer.

The younger raises his hand aloft—and now the murmurs cease, the daggers are returned to their sheaths, and marvel takes the place of audible suspicion.

The old man casts his eyes around the mighty throng, but masks—masks—

masks greet his vision on every hand. His cheek is pale with suffering, not fear. His limbs are tremulous, and his lips in vain essay to speak.

His younger and more hardy companion leads him to a seat on the right of the altar, and, like a son humouring the whims of a feeble-minded parent, fears not, in sight of a thousand eyes, to do each little act which gives relief or feeds the humour of his sire. And now that kindness is acknowledged by the throng, for lo! how lustily they shout.

The hand of the mask is raised again—the assemblage is dumb.

Hark! to the voice of the swayer of the multitude.

"Venetians, ye must not deem me faithless to the post which ye have honoured me with, because of the lateness of my arrival at this our last, most solemn meeting. But when ye have heard the cause of my detention, ye will pardon my lateness. Ye know well the features of yon old man—ye have known, ye have felt his kindness, justice, and humanity for years, when the dark power, for whose destruction we are now assembled, held over us the hidden steel and midnight summons. Look on him, pity him, for he hath suffered,—welcome him, for I bring him to ye as a candidate for your voices.

"For the last five days, he hath suffered the infernal torments which only the fiends of Venice are capable of inflicting upon man. On a base, false, and cowardly charge he was summoned at midnight, by the dark messenger of the tribunal to appear before the 'Ten' and answer to charges which none but a devil could invent. He was tried, condemned, and sentenced to the 'sulphur death.' Venetians, he is your doge—ye are his loyal subjects, and now, fresh from the dungeon's torture, he comes to join us in our battle with the foes of liberty and conscience. Shall he be one of us? it is for your voices to decide whether our cause shall be aided by the influence and worth of one so potent as our doge.'

"Who will vouch for his honesty?" demanded a voice in the throng.

"Galliano," responded the noble, boldly.

A look of gratitude from the aged victim rewarded the young noble's generosity.

"Shall he be one of us?" demanded Galliano energetically; "shall we proceed in the coming struggle with a star at our side, whose fame as a warrior, a statesman, and a man hath never been excelled by the brightest of our country's sons? Shall we go forth, with this brave man and true, this great man and good, this sage and warrior, at our head, or shall we, trusting to his honour and fidelity, let him depart, to be again seized by the dark tribunal, a victim to its rapacity. It is for you to say whether he shall become one of us, and live; or, return to the vengeance of the 'Ten,' and die!"

The assembly was silent.

"Your signal, friends, your signal," cried the noble.

Every right hand of the throng was raised aloft.

"Enough, friends—I thank ye." Then turning to the pale doge, the noble added—"Father of Venice, Jacopo the Just. it is the pleasure of these worthy citizens that you be admitted into our holy cause. Thou wilt now prepare to take the initiatory oath; it is a solemn and a holy one, and he who breaks it, forfeits all right to honour, manhood, yea, and life. Art thou willing to run such hazard?"

"I am," replied the old man, firmly.

"Then arise, and take thy stand with me beside this altar."

The doge obeyed.

"Lay thy hand upon this holy volume," added the noble, "and follow me in the oath."

"By all my hopes of life on earth—by all the ties that bind me to kindred, friends and country—by all my hopes of heaven and fears of hell—I swear to be faithful and true to the cause of which I am a brother; to hold myself in readiness to follow the orders of my officers; to aid my brother members when in suffering or in danger; to be ready at all hours, whenever summoned, to carry out the object of our institution—to keep secret its secrets, to keep secret its proceedings, to keep secret the names of its members, to keep secret its place of meeting—to advance its power, influence, and number by every means in the power of my hands, mind, and tongue ; to give of my means and abundance all that can be given, to sustain and stfengthen our institution ; to obey when ordered, though it were to sacrifice my dearest friends, my kindred in blood, or though it were to jeopardise mine own life ; to obey its officers, though to obey were peril beyond conception :   This do I swear, in sight of heaven and earth, and will maintain my oath before the courts of Life, Death. or Darkness !

Word for word, with trembling lips, he followed the speaker, till the last word of the fearful and responsible oath was uttered.

Then advanced the secretary with his ledger.   Laying it on the altar, he opened its pages, saying,—

"Thy name ?"

"For what ?" demanded the doge.

"This book doth bear the name of every member of our order, signed, or marked, by his own hand," responded the secretary.

"Give me the pen," said the duke, huskily.

It was put into his hand.

Why paused he ? His son was one of the creatures of the "Ten"—the "Ten' were terrible in their decrees, terrible in their tortures—but his son was allied to them—if the "tTen" were destroyed, his son, his darling, spoiled, but yet his son, would be swept away with them.   He had suffered by both, terribly suffered— but he was a father, and had a father's feelings.   E'en now, if his Leonardo stood before him, for all his wickedness of heart, he felt he could forgive him wholly, yea, heartily forgive him.   Though his son had forgot his duties, his loyalty, his manliness, his affection, still there was yet a pleader for him in his father s heart. He knew his boy to be marked—that many a heart in that throng thirsted for his blood, and would have it—and yet he, a father, was about to join a band of men whose solemn purpose was to slay, in cold blood, suddenly, and at midnight, the protectors of his son.   He felt his eyes grow dim—he could not see the book before him, his hand trembled.

"Why dost thou pause ?" said the noble.

The lips of the doge moved, but no sound issued forth.

"The torture hath done its work upon him," thought the noble.

"He fears to sign, but he has taken the oath," shouted a voice.

"He must sign, or die, doge or no doge," shouted another.

"Aye, he must," echoed an hundred voices, at once.

"Silence !" thundered Galliano, indignantly ; "think ye the old man means us treachery ?   For shame !   Scarce two hours have flown, since I with the conni- vance of one of the tribunal's instruments, rescued him, stealthily, from the dungeon where he was to linger till murdered by the torture !   Last night the tribunal stretched him on the rack to extort confession.   'Tis the agony of his tortured limbs that now makes him pause.   His strength is gone.   Would you add to his sufferings by harsh, unkind reproaches ?"

The throng was silent.

The old man leaned against the altar, and, casting a look of gratitude upon his defender, said, feebly—"Cease thy pleading, noble youth ; I am not popular with these stern men, and thy efforts will be of little or no avail .   My hours are well nigh numbered,—my aid in your cause feeble, no matter how heartily given.   Still, go on ; go on, with an old man's dying blessing.   Rid Venice of its plague—sweep them off, and be freemen once more.   Posterity will do your efforts justice, whether fruitless or successful.   If you succeed, go at once to an election and create your doge.   Let the people's choice live and reign for the people ; not for himself, but for the great body of Venice, I—I—."

His voice had now sunk to a whisper.   Galliano rushed toward and supported him from falling.

The secretary ran, and throwing the old man's right shoulder over his neck, sustained him on one side, as the young noble did the same on the other.

The doge then turning his face toward the throng, and, running his eyes over the multitude, as if to command their attention, said, in a tone feeble, but whisperingly udible, " Venetians, I have not enough of life in me to aid your cause physically; fresh from the torture house of the tribunal, with the effects of the rack now hastening me into the dark house of the lifeless, I can attest how high and how holy is the cause which has for its object the entire destruction of so dark and terrible a power. I implore you to put a period to this fiendish tribunal. Its acts for an hundred years, as the archives of our royal library all attest, have been of the most remorseless and fiendish character—its dark pall falling alike on the tender maid, as on the time-hued matron : sparing none, but with mocking trials, and relentless tortures, hurrying all into the dark shades of the eternities. Shall this be longer borne, and we be called Venetians? No; let us arise in our might, and, with one purpose, one thought, free ourselves from such cowardly dastards, such bloodthirsty fiends. Their houses of torture are well known to this gallant gentleman beside me, whose strong heart and fearless arm rescued me from the death-cell. He knows their dark avenues and mazes, their mysterious doors and hidden traps, and can lead you through all their labyrinths as unerringly as if he had traversed them since childhood. Let him be your guide. And, if an old man"s prayer can aught avail, let him be your leader, too ; a more faithful, a keener, a bolder cannot be found on earth."

A burst of applause here informed the venerable speaker that the sentiments of the throng were in unison with his own.

The duke proceeded, in a tone firmer than before :

" The counsels of your leader must be obeyed ; no murmurs must ascend to discourage, no deeds performed other than he has ordered, to baulk his purposes. Be firm, courageous, and fear not ; in the hour ye choose for the attempt, let no thought of fear enter your breast ; but let each man strike as if a world's existence depended on his bravery. ¶ Ask Heaven's aid on your enterprise, and fear not but the succeeding dawn will break on the overthrow of the tribunal, and be the birth hour of our freedom !"

Scarce had he finished, when a spontaneous shot from the huge throng, rang through the vault, and voices shouted, " Foscari ! Foscari! be one of us ! be one of us !"

Over exertion, in his address, had weakened the doge, and he could scarcely master himself sufficiently to bow his thanks. He seized the pen, and, with a trembling hand, added his name, to the long list : at sight of which, loud bursts of cheers again rang through the vault, and voices shouted—" Foscari ! Foscari ! Fascari the Just ! he is one of us—he is one of us !"

When the enthusiasm of the throng had somewhat abated, the President of the Patriots took his seat, and, with a little hammer, called all to silence ; and then called on the secretary for the list of new members. This being done, the latter were summoned to the altar, and there, hand in hand, the foremost having his hand upon the book, the formalities of initiation were gone through, and the rostrum was again cleared.

The general history of the institution was then read by the secretary; all its transactions, the amount of funds loaned to arm and support its members in the coming struggle; the number of its members, and all and everything pertaining to its transactions. Speeches were made to strengthen and encourage the timid ; warnings were given to intimidate the doubtful, if any such were there. The place of gathering on the following night appointed ; a benediciction, by the doge, was pronounced ; and ten minutes afterwards, the vault was all dark, all silent.

CHAPTER XVI.

THE NIGHT OF THE CARNIVAL.

THE skies were dark and starless ; the night queen, as if in anger, shed neither ray nor light upon the earth ; a gloomy, solemn darkness pervaded the isles scattered over the broad Adriatic ! the waters were still as if the Eternal's voice had turned it into dark and solid glass ; the atmosphere was deadly calm and hot.

The piers of Venice were crowded with continually arriving boats from the numerous isles around ; the streets were thronged with citizens and strangers, all attended by servants bearing flambeaux, and all hurrying towards St. Mark's Square. Torches and lamps festooned, hung beneath the windows of every house; music, from a thousand instruments, greeted the comers, now issuing from every corner in the square.

The street, from side to side, was floored with close-grooved planks, and rendered as slippery as glass by holistone ; and cautious was the foot that did not fall. Shoes, sandals, boots, slippers, and chopines, were chalked by the knowing ones ; while those who visited the scene for the first time, afforded great diversion by their numerous falls, and awkward attempts to preserve their equilibrium.

The sports commenced by the entrance of a hundred morris dancers, all dressed in tight-fitting pantaloons and jackets, with numerous small bells attached to their steeple caps and belted waists. Their grotesque dance being finished, and confidence implanted in the breasts of the over-modest, the hilarity of the carnival began. Clowns, sober citizens, monkeys, villagers, tigers, usurers, and monks, all joined in one mirthful set, each figure dancing, as closely as possible, in imitation of the thing whose character he represented.

The heat was oppressive, and cunning wights, taking advantage of the holitime, carried about water, and choice wines, for which receiving whatever they demanded, they made enough to pay for the time lost in preparing, and the expense incurred in costuming for the gay holitime.

Nuns with everything but nun-like steps, might be seen, arm-in-arm, with a soldier ; a tiger with a monkey on his back, the monkey doing the roaring part, and the tiger, both through mistake, performing the monkey's squeak; a burly monk with huge chops, and laughter-loving eyes, dancing a comic couplet with a gay shepherdess ; a king footing it with a huge, greasy looking cook ; and ten thousand other fantastic and laughable vagaries might be witnessed, as the sports and crowd increased.

The bell of St. Mark's temple struck the midnight signal ; and, ere its sound had died away, the darkness was changed to the light of day, by the sudden discharge of a thousand rockets, from all parts of the torch-lit square. This lasted for about five minutes, in which time a countless host of caps were raised aloft on poles, and swung round in the air, amidst deafening shouts.

Pedlers of food, and wine, and water were now seen busily disposing of their articles to the hungry and thirsty, while the thousand antics of the merry throng kept the pave alive with boisterous delight.

A tall form stood at the door of a two-story house, opposite the temple of St. Mark, scanning, with scowling brows, the figures of the merry multitude. The house before which he stood had nothing in it to distinguish it from the buildings on either side of it, except, indeed, that its facade was humbler in its pretensions. It was an ordinary building, and free from all the fancy of stucco and carved work which distinguished the majority of the buildings in St. Mark's Square. It appeared to be the residence of some wealthy, but unpretending citizen, and had nothing to recommend it to the passing eye, but its simplicity. The individual alluded to was young in years, gay in his habiliments, handsome in figure and features, and evidently one who had no small opinion of his own importance.

His eyes were everywhere; but an eye was on him, that he little dreamt of; an eye, dark, large, sharp, and piercing as his own. Having satisfied his curiosity, and growing tired of gazing on sports in which neither his humour nor pride would permit him to mingle, he opened the door cautiously, though in an apparently careless manner, and disappeared. Whether he had received a signal, invisible to all but himself, to hurry him from the scene where he was only a spectator, or whether he retired to avoid the eye or presence of some approaching foe, it matters not —he retired, and, a few moments afterward, a fancy masque was being played almost in front of the house, which was so attractive, that hundreds, aye hundreds on hundreds, gathered around to witness it.

They gathered around to witness the mask, we say; but many, instead of remaining to feast their eyes upon the farce, gradually drew back, and one by one, disappeared through the very door which the personage before mentioned had entered. The mirth of the masque was at its height—the spectators were splitting their sides with laughter—their eyes were bent upon each feature of the gay performance, when, lo! hundreds fell back, just as unpropped earth gives way before the press of dampness, and approached the open door. They disappeared rapidly, and when the masque was over, the remaining auditors were astonished at the thinness of their number. They imagined that the play they had been looking on was poor, and that the greater part of its auditors had retired in disgust; and so, likewise people, they left the spot too, in order that they might not be reproached with gazing delightedly upon a play of *parvenu* caste!

CHAPTER XVII.

THE DUNGEONS OF THE TRIBUNAL.

THE trial chamber of the tribunal was about sixty feet in length, thirty in width, and about sixteen feet high. The walls and ceiling were lined with black silk velvet, ornamented (or disfigured, if you will), with silver emblems of the different modes of torture used by the council to extort confession, or silence the breathings of its victims. Near the head of the apartment stood an altar, covered with the same dark material, the front of which was garnished with a silvery cross, woven into the cloth. A semi-circular seat ran round the altar, on which the members of the tribunal sat when deliberating, or holding council on their victims. In its centre was an upraised chair, for the president, and before it, lying on the altar, an open book, a naked dagger, and materials for writing. At either end of the altar stood a table, covered with parchments and writing materials; while directly before it stood a circular paling of iron, for prisoners when on trial. A huge lamp, hung from the ceiling, over the pailing, whose bright light was calculated to fall directly upon the person of the prisoner. A rack, with all its infernal apparatus, was visible, a few paces from the altar.

Such was the trial chamber, when its members were absent. But on the night of the carnival, it was tenanted, and hideous was the sight it presented. A white haired man, haggard and pale, stood in the prisoner's dock!—Chains on his hands, and chains on his feet; a pulley hung from the ceiling, the hook of which ran through an iron circle attached to the back of a broad, thick, leathern belt, which girded the waist of the prisoner; the end of this pulley was in the hands of a couple of fierce looking wretches, garbed in coarse dark frocks, reaching to their knees.   The tribunal was sitting, each member bare headed, masked, and domi-noed.   The lamp before mentioned, threw a broad, bright light over the features of the half naked prisoner, over the bright trappings of the velveted wa and ceil-ing, over the parchments and altar and rack, and over the glossy masks and domi-noes of the judges.

"Jacopo Foscari," said he, who sat in the president's chair, "what hast thou to say to the charge urged against thee ?"

"Not guilty," responded the prisoner.

"Not guilty ?" repeated the judge, in apparent amazement.   "We have a wit-ness against you."

"Produce him," said the prisoner.

"Behold him," said the president, pointing to one of the council, who had just rise n from his seat.

"Doth he accuse me?" demanded the prisoner, faintly.

"He doth," responded the president.

"Of murder ?"

"Of murder."

"Hath he sworn it ?"

"He hath."

"He hath spoken falsely, sirs. Jacopo Foscari arraigns him for falsehood and perjury."

"Thou are thyself arraigned, doge, and it behoves thee to rid thyself of the charges against thee, ere thou attemptest to bear witness against another. Thou art accused of the foul murder of Uberoni, the rich usurer, for the sake of his sup-posed wealth. Sentence hath been passed upon thee. Why should it not be per-formed !"

"Ye have the power, dark men, as ye are," said the prisoner, boldly, "ye have the power of murder in your hand, and ye may use it on me, soon as it consorts with your will; but I am innocent, and sith there is no means of baffling ye in your humour for my blood, e'en take my life : 'twill be but another to the already long list of your crimes."

"Beware, rash man," exclaimed the president, "less impertinence in thy speech would perhaps incline us to mercy."

"Mercy ! your mercy?" cried the prisoner, in tones of the most withering scorn ; "ye showed it me two nights agone, when, upon this same false charge, ye stretched me on yon rack, and, after glutting your sanguinary eyes upon my tor-tures, ye bade your slaves release and plunge me back into the dungeon from whence ye took me. Your mercy ! the mercy of the 'Ten !' Ha ! ha ! ha ! "

"Madman !" exclaimed the president, "dost beard us to our very throats ! Ho! there, ye knaves! lay him on the rack!   Wrench him limb from limb ? We'll see if his proud heart cannot be broken, or his unbridled tongue taught reverence and decency in its speech !"

As the minions of the tribunal obeyed the order of the president, he who had stood up as witness against the doge, was seen to start and heard to groan as if an earthquake had suddenly opened before him. A hand of one beside him was laid gently upon his shoulder, and his presence of mind returning, he resumed his former seeming stolidity.

"Now," continued the president, rising, and gazing upon his victim, as he lay tretched upon the iron bed, "confess the means by which thou didst escape thy dungeon yesternight, and thou shalt escape the torture."

The prisoner was silent.

"Confess the name of thy accomplice, and thou shalt be pardoned the murder of the usurer," continued the president.

Still the prisoner uttered not a word.

"Confess, ere I give the sign," thundered the president.

"I laugh at thee and thy threats, villain," responded the prisoner.

The council rose in agitation, and hastily collected round the prostrate man.

In faith, they had good cause for trembling; a traitor was within their gates, or else the secret of the entrance to their dungeons was known to some daring one unknown to the tribunal. He, the doge, their last and highest victim, had found some secret means of escaping his dungeon; true, they had re-captured him, at dawn, as he was stealing, with a companion, through a bye-path, near St. Mark's

cathedral, into the rear of the gardens of the ducal palace; still, the secret of the entrance was known to another than themselves. The fact troubled them, and to find out the name of the being possessing this mighty and dangerous secret, caused the tribunal to dally with their victim ere they resorted to the last deadly measure.

"Confess, and save thy life," said the president; "give us but the name of
No. 10.

him our spies found thee with this morn, and thou shalt live. Refuse, and thou shalt die."

"Do your worst—I'll betray no man," replied the prisoner firmly.

"Beware! our vengeance is ——"

"Laughed at, and at end," thundered a voice, without.

A moment more, and a knight, in black armour, his vizor down, his sword drawn, and accompanied by a hundred warriors, in mail, each bearing a broad, bright blade in his right hand, entered the chamber, and confronted the astonished tribunal.

"Ho, there! what treachery is this?" cried the president, starting back.

"No treachery, villains!" replied the black knight; "we are Venetians, and your doomsmen! Seize them!" he added, pointing to his companions.

"Stand back, knaves!" cried one of the judges, rushing forward, his sword drawn, and throwing off his domino, "stand back, as ye do value life! Give we but the signal, ye are on all sides hemmed in, and death, death in its most startling and terrible shape, is your portion. Think ye to come and beard us thus in our very den? Fly, fools, fly, and save your wretched lives!"

"Cease, thou foul-mouthed braggart! cease thine empty vauntings, for every passage, or entrance to this bloody chamber is filled with men thirsting for your blood! Think'st thou, by this shallow trick, to intimidate hearts a thousand times more brave and cunning than thine own? Fool! thou art too well begirt, though armies could now spring up on all sides of this chamber to aid thee—death, death, in its most appalling forms, have been marked out for thee and all thy fellow assassins! Seize them!"

The knights obeyed; and, in five minutes, every member of the tribunal, together with the wretches who were about to strangle the aged man on the rack, were seized, bound and tied to the altar around which they had so often sat in sanguinary council.

"Behold, my friends," cried the black knight, pointing to the rack, "behold the weapons of these midnight murderers. Behold the fearful engines we are called upon by reason, manhood, justice, aye, and fate, to destroy. Release yon noble victim, and bear him to the palace. We'll hear his thanks another time," he continued with averted face, as the doge, freed from his iron manacles, was about to throw himself on his knees and thank his deliverers, for their timely arrival; "we'll hear his thanks another time. Bear him hence, and see him well attended, ere ye quit your burden. Away!"

"And now," continued the knight, "pass the word for the oil, we'll teach these idle hounds the mercy they have taught to others."

The oil was brought.

"Now, sirs," said the black knight, turning to the judges, "it is but the emptying of these jars upon this pave, and the touching of this torch to the oil, and ye are in a human hell, built by your own death-dealing hands. What if we so act?"

The judges were silent.

"What if, like yourselves, we, to satisfy our thirst for blood, fire these dungeons, leaving you, partners in blood and iniquity, to list to each other's cries and shrieks and groans, as the flames of vengeance hurry ye from this chamber of fire into that burning lake the other side the eternities which ye so long have laughed at?"

"Do it," said one of the judges, sullenly; "we fear not."

"Liar that thou art," replied the knight, "'tis thy fear that gives thee this sad show of courage in the dark hour of death. Are ye then so brave, that ye will not ask for mercy? Ho, there!" he added, turning to his men, "swathe these walls with oil. We'll e'en burn the villains into a crisp."

A cry of terror, rose from the midst of the captive judges, as they beheld the threat of their unknown captor being carried into effect.

"What! ye come to your senses at last, eh?" exclaimed the knight, with a derisive laugh; "ye begin at last to have a foretaste of the dark doom which ye have so oft inflicted upon your wretched victims? Ho, there! my brave hea^{rts}, seize these dastards, and convey them to the outer vault."

His command was obeyed.

"Now then, friends," continued the knight, "pass the word, to set all the captives free, swathe all the dungeons with oil and pitch, and when we reach the outer vault, let the torch fire the dungeons—if possible, we'll end our glorious work without shedding a drop of human blood."

The dungeons were opened, and captive after captive released, till not a cell was left unexplored. The walls, floors, and ceilings were then bedaubed with oil and pitch, and all moved, hastily, to the outward vault. There the judges stood, chained, and, devoid of their cloaks, gazing sullenly on their captors,—their faces were well known, and the huge throng recognised many a favourite citizen among the now powerless judges.

The black knight advanced towards one who bore a torch, and seizing it, cried out—"Seize these villains, and bear them to the ducal hall. Away, on your lives —for the brand must now end these scenes of blood!"

None needed a second bidding; and making a rush for the stair flight, were, with their captives, soon beyond the reach of danger. The knight finding himself alone, flung the burning torch into the narrow passage; and for a moment paused to witness the result. The passage, swathed with oil and pitch, was instantaneously in a flame, and spreading like a sea of fire, till all before him was of one lurid glow. The heat drove him to the stair flight, where stood a large jar of pitch and oil. A slight push sent it into the vault, where it was soon caught by the approaching fire. The danger was now evident, and, closing the door, the black knight ran, with his few remaining companions, up stairs. A crowd was congregated without the door; which, on the approach of our hero, soon gave way, and all bent their steps towards the palace.

In a square phalanx they moved, the black knights in the centre, till they reached the ducal mansion.

CHAPTER XVIII.

THE TRIAL.

THE reception hall of the ducal palace was filled to overflowing. An oaken desk, carved in the fashion of the furniture of the middle ages, stood in the upper end of the hall. Behind it, his vizor off, and his manly face exposed to the full view of the multitude, sat Galliano, the hero of the night. Ranged on either side, were twenty knights in black armour, each holding his helmet on his arm before his breast. On either end of the desk stood a large waxen taper, flinging a broad light around. The captive judges were in a line before the desk, their faces towards the desk, and separated from the spectators by an iron railing, which ran from side to side of the apartment. Silence reigned throughout the hall.

"Venetians," said Galliano, in a stern voice, "the late foes of our beloved country, are now before you for judgment. The witnesses against them are your own eyes, and the sufferings which we all have endured since nature gave us breath. Are ye prepared for judgment?"

"We are," was the reply, as with one voice.

"Their crimes are known to ye—their villany as plainly graven on your hearts, as the memory of yesterday. Speak, what is the doom of the prisoners?"

"Death!" was the solemn response.

"Without shriving—without preparation?"

" Without shriving—without preparation !"

" Their mode of death ?"

" The block—the block !"

" When, and where ?"

" This hour, and in front of the church of St. Mark !"

" Who shall be their executioner?"

" Their chief," was the reply again, as with one voice.

' Ho, there !" exclaimed the black knight, rising from his seat, " let the hall be cleared ; and let the state block and axe, which have lain so long unused, be brought and placed on the portico of St. Mark's.   It is decreed!"

The hall was cleared of all save the knights and their prisoners.

Galliano whispered to his companions ; on which two of them hastily left the apartment by a side door.

Silence reigned there some half hour ; at the expiration of which time, the knights returned, accompanied by a grey haired priest and a mantled female.

Galliano led the latter behind an oaken desk. She trembled, and would have sunk, had not the arm of the noble sustained her.

" Courage, fair lady," he whispered ; " courage, or else our pains will all be turned to naught.   Command thy nerves with all thy might ; harm cannot come to thee, surrounded as thou art by those who know thy melancholy history well, and who would die for thee.   Courage !"

She answered not, but bent her head upon his arm, and wept.

The noble made a sign to those who had brought the lady, and they advanced; resigning the female to their charge, Galliano fixed his eye upon one of the captives, and said, in a deep and solemn tone, " Leonardo Foscari—on the verge of eternity, as thou art, I summon thee in Heaven's name, to do one act of justice, which will, in part, redeem the infamy thou hast brought upon thy father's name."

' What is it ?" demanded Foscari, sullenly.

" Behold this tender form," said the noble, turning and pointing as he spoke " and let thy once noble heart answer thee."

" I am no reader of riddles," replied the roue, sneeringly.

" Nor need'st thou be, to draw the meaning I would have thee," said the noble, stifling his anger at the insolent reply.   " Lead him hither ?" he added, addressing the knights near the prisoners.

The roue made no resistance.

" What think'st thou now ?" said the noble, lifting aside the veil which had hidden the features of the female.

" Eugenia !" exclaimed the roue, starting back at the pale countenance of his weeping victim.

" The same," said the noble, indignantly ; " Eugenia, the orange girl of Venice ! She, whom thy false tongue did first betray and afterwards malign. Behold her now, pale with misery and woe—behold her now, heart-broken, as thou hast made her ! "

"Well, sir, the object of bringing us again together?" said the roue, with a sneer, and recovering his self-possession.

" To urge thee to do her justice," replied the noble, indignantly.

" As how, my gallant lord ?"

" By wedding her, ere thou diest," responded Galliano.

The roue laughed.

" Hast thou no heart?" said a feeble voice near him.

Foscari turned pale and started—his sire was before him—his sire, pale with suffering in limb and brain.

" Hast thou no heart ?" repeated the doge, in a low, feeble, sad, reproachful voice ; " hast thou no heart, Leonardo ?"

The roue heard the tones of that voice, and saw the mighty change in that face, whose features almost till now were ever turned on him with parental love and pride.   He shrank as he gazed, he trembled at the changed tones of that voice, as they fell upon his ear—changed, too, by his own ingrate heart.

" On the verge of that dread eternity, where we soon shall meet together," con-untied the doge, " I implore thee to do what thou canst, whilst yet the breath is in thee, by righting this poor girl. · Lo! death is near at hand, boy, and if thou'lt but do this one little act of justice, thy father's lips will pronounce his pardon for thy guilt towards him, and his last prayer shall ascend to Heaven for mercy on thy soul! Wilt thou do it?"

Leonardo replied not.

" Hast thou no spark of manliness nor honour left in thee, boy?" said the doge, in a choked voice. " Shall thy poor father go down into his grave with the con-viction that his only begotten shamed the mother's breast that bore him? Speak, Leonardo,—my boy—one word! See, thy poor sire is on his knees before thee!"

The eyes of the roue were moistened—his lips trembled—his frame shook—he spoke no word, but *his sire had conquered.*

The roue raised his father kindly up—then sank at his father's feet—then seized his father's hands in his, and implored his forgiveness.

" When thou hast righted her thou hast wronged!" said the old man, solemnly.

At this moment, the solemn tongue of St. Mark's steeple tolled a solitary chime.

The doge staggered against the desk—his face ashy, his eyes turned upward, and his lips murmuring—" O God!"

" The block is prepared—the axe whetted," said a solemn voice, at the door.

What is that glossy stream now coursing down the old man's cheeks—tears, silent ones?

The roue advanced to the orange girl, and taking her hand, said, in a low, deep voice—

" Eugenia, thy hand is cold and icy; unlike the hand which, in days long gone, I used to hold in mine without a sigh or murmur from thy lips: it is cold now, as thy betrayer's soon will be. I did thee foul and heartless wrong, for which, on the threshold of eternity, I implore thy pardon and the forgiveness of thy kindred. The priest is at hand to seal my repentance—let him approach, that my last act on earth may not add to the remorse which burns within this heart."

The ceremony commenced, went on, was finished.

Again, St. Mark's bell rang a warning note.

" The prisoners are summoned to the block," said the voice at the door.

" Let this my first, my last honest kiss, Eugenia," said the roue in a brusque tone, " be the pledge of my repentance." Then rushing to his father, he knelt, and, seizing the old man's listless hand, exclaimed—" Father! father! *now* forgive and bless me!"

The lips of the doge moved, but nought save a whispering sound was heard.

" Father! father! for God's sake! speak to me!" repeated the roue in agony.

His father's eyes were raised heavenward—his lips were moving, as if in prayer.

The bell pealed again.

" The hour for death is struck," said the voice.

The roue started up—embraced his unconscious sire—then waving a farewell to his new made bride, sprang into the procession of judges, as guarded on either side, by the black knights, they slowly left the hall.

The doge, the priest, the orange girl and one in the garb of a gondolier alone remained. The lips and eyes of the doge still heavenward turned; the priest and gondolier supporting the statue-like form of the veiled bride.

The bell struck again; a sound as of an axe falling on a block, grated on their ears. A long loud shriek rang through the hall—the orange girl fell back.

Shouts swelled in the square, as the last stroke of the executioner's axe fell on the block, and cries, wild and solemn—and shrill and enthusiastic, split the air—" The tyrants are slain—Venice is free!"

With that loud shout, the lips of the doge ceased to move—his eyes grew glassy—his limbs tottered, and his spirit was travelling with that of his son to the Soul's High Court.

CHAPTER XIX.

THE DAWN OF FREEDOM.

THE news of the execution flew from mouth to mouth, like wildfire ; the people looked in each others' eyes half paralysed ; even those who had been in the conspiracy could scarce believe their glorious work was fully accomplished, till they beheld the decapitated trunks of those who had composed the tribunal. The carnival ceased, only to break forth anew with wilder mirth. People laughed, danced, shouted, yea, and wept for gladness' sake. Groups met, chatted a moment over the affair, then separated, in wild joy, and, collecting again together, rehearsed their former converse. So wild the enthusiasm, that old men, forgetting their age, frolicked, danced, gambolled, shouted, and made merry, like youths ; misers forgot their avarice, and joining in the general gladsomeness, squandered the savings of years; processions formed in every part of the city, and preceded by music, strode through Venice in triumph. The sick and the feeble, the halt and the blind, were helped to the windows that they might either see the cavalcade, or hear the enthusiastic strains which announced their country's freedom from the thrall of the long-dreaded. The timid forgot their timidity, and, as they strode in the processions, felt brave as the bravest ; the niggard forgot his narrow-heartedness, and when the upraised hand of the beggar met his regenerated eye, gave of his means freely ; men who had long been foes, met, and in the patriotism of their hearts, looked kindly on each other, and embraced ; jealousies were forgotten by rival tradesmen, and free and generous hands and sympathies exchanged, and lasting friendships formed where all before was hatred. It was a time of universal joy, and brought back to the mental eye of the moralist, those happy days and scene when men's faces were the outward pictures of their hearts.

Still there was a sadness, too, in Venice—the corse of the just doge,—Foscari, —lay in state in the ducal palace. Waxen tapers gleamed around the bier, and monks, and priests, and the dignitaries of the state sat in little groups thinking of the dead. Alone in his palace with no son nor wife nor daughter to weep o'er his pale and deathly brow, lay Jacopo the Just. None wept for him—none told his virtues, his secret deeds of charity, or his worth. Men of place and mammon were around him, gazing on his shroud, and thinking of their future in regard to place and mammon. They knew their country was freed from a yoke which had, in its time, bowed all their necks to its will ; but they participated not in the general joy, because the doge's death and the tribunal's overthrow might be the harbingers only of their loss of office. And in this train of thought around the bier of death, they pondered o'er the means of coining gold and a place. "Who shall be the next doge? Who be the electors? Shall my office and its emoluments be wrested from me? Or shall I become a favourite with the elected one? Such were a few of the thousand interrogatories each of the sitters put to himself, while paying one of the last duties of man to his fellow man in that hall where death rejoiced o'er one victim.

But there were many on that day whose minds were sorely rent reflecting on the state of things which had been brought about by the conspirators. The doge was dead—this was not expected, and no provision had been made for such emergency.

A party of twenty men were assembled in St. Mary's vault. Their ages varied from thirty to fifty years. They were of different castes in rank, and each was guarded as befitted his rank and calling. They were sitting in solemn conclave, upon the rostrum and around the altar on which they had before sworn to immolate the tyrannical rulers of their country. They were the officers of the sworn brotherhood. They had been in council since daybreak, and had not broken bread nor tasted drink, nor closed their eyes in slumber since the hour of their entrance into the dungeons of the late tribunal. It was now verging on to noon, and they had not yet decided on the object of their meeting.

When the council had broken up, a glow of earnest satisfaction was visible in every eye and on every cheek ; and on the day succeeding the burial of the late doge, the anxieties and cares of those who had held office under him were set at rest for ever : and—they murmured !

CHAPTER XX.

THE BRIDAL MORN.

PASS we now three months.

It was about the hour of nine, on a lovely morning in June, that a young man, in the garb of a secretary, knocked briskly at the door of a humble and retired-looking dwelling in the Raoni Square. He wore a small moustache, a pointed beard and jetty ringlets hung over his shoulders. A slender rapier hung at his side, and a short dagger dangled from his girdle. He was handsome as the term goes, and—we are afraid to believe—knew it. There was a no small share of importance in his step, and carriage ; but then he was young. He entered, *sans monie*, and was met in the hall by a young lady, whom we have already introduced to the reader.

" You are one to keep a promise !" said the young lady tossing her head indignantly.

" Nay, I could not come earlier," replied the secretary ; " but we shall lose nothing by this trifling delay, for I have the doge's permission to take thee to the palace, that we may enter St. Mark's with the bridal cortege. So get thee ready as soon as may be."

There was a mischievous light in the eyes of the secretary during this brief speech.

They entered the sitting room.

" Ho ! ho !" said the secretary, as his eyes fell on some bright and gauzy ornaments which were lying on a cushion in one corner.

The maiden met his glance and blushed. She did not speak a syllable, blushed to the temples. A great deal of meaning is often conveyed in a blush.

" Nay, thou shalt wear it, my beloved," said the secretary, taking her hand and drawing her fondly to his breast, and imprinting a lover's seal upon her lips. " So, like a fair and bewitching damsel, don it with all speed."

Did she need a second bidding ?

Ten minutes afterward, they left the house, and bent their steps in the direction of the palace.

St. Mark's temple was crowded with the wives and daughters and scions of all castes in Venice. From the palace to the church was but a short distance ; but that short distance was amply taken advantage of by the populace, and a crowd was collected from either side of the palace portals, to either side of the portals of the church, leaving a broad and winding passage for the noble cortege.

The bell of St. Mark's pealed forth merrily, and its notes seemed to spread joyousness over the hearts and faces of the multitude. The bridal bells, the bridal bells, how merrily they rang !

The palace portals were opened wide, and the gaping throng shouted as if their lungs would crack, as the bridal procession appeared.

" Make way—make way !" shouted the guards who had been posted to keep clear the passage to the temple. The throng fell back, but not unwillingly—for there was not one in that mighty throng, but would have died, if necessary, in defence of the well-beloved doge.

A party of priests and altar attendants led the procession ; a score of pages following them, and the different grades of the nobility after them, till the doge in his bridal robes appeared. Then rang the echoing air with shouts and *vivas* and waving of caps, and kerchiefs, by the multitude. The doge bowed his thanks, and his noble bearing and splendid figure well became his office, as the whispers of admiration, as he passed, well attested Almost next him, followed Calvari, secretary to the doge, leading a young and blushing maiden, Junetta by name ; and so firm and confident was his step that many believed he had no right to the blushing one at his side. He appeared to be too confident in his carriage for a lover ; so thought and so spoke the ladies. He bore himself like a true and fearless man ; so thought and so spoke the men. The procession had reached and entered the church ; still the bells rang merrily—but where was the bride? So questioned the multitude without, so did not question the multitude within : for the bride, veiled, had entered by the vestry door, even at the moment her future lord had entered by the front. The broad aisle was cleared for the bridegroom and his party, and the bride and bridegroom met, as if by accident—but it was not by accident—and then they strode solemnly, (people put on such solemn airs !) to a royal seat, prepared for them on the right hand of the marble altar. The secretary and his beloved were not far off, and the parents and cousins of Junetta, by a strange coincidence, were not far away from their daughter. Every body looked grave, and almost every one blushed, although there was but little need of either. These things will happen, despite of their impropriety !

The bell ceased pealing, and ere the cadence of its last note had died away, the bride and bridegroom were summoned by the priest, and the doge, Galliano, and his beloved Isabel were united for ever. The ring was placed upon the finger of the bride, and then St. Mark's temple re-echoed to the shouts of those within and the cheering of those without. The bell pealed again, and even it seemed to share in the silvery joy, so silvery were its notes.

Another couple passed the ordeal of the priest, and they were cheered too, but not so loudly as the noble pair that preceded them ; still they were cheered, and a little old man and a little old woman were observed to be very fussy, and nervous during the ceremony ; weeping and smiling by turns, and turning to the people and motioning them to be silent, as if they had been the cheered ones, and were more important than they were. How people will act sometimes !

As the doge was leaving the church to return to the palace, his eye was observed to look anxiously around, as if in search of faces that had not yet met his eye. An expression of sadness passed athwart his brow, as if disappointed in his search.

CHAPTER XXI.

CONCLUSION.

ON a low cushioned couch, in a chamber where the luxuries of the higher caste contrasted strongly with the simple garniture of the lowly, reclined the fragile form of the fair but suffering Eugenia. The apartment had but one window, and that was adorned with a curtain of crimson gauze. It was mid-day ; and the sun-rays gleaming through the curtain, cast a glowing tint upon the couch on which the

orange girl reclined.   Her head was leaning upon her upraised hand, and her
dark eyes gazing vacantly upon the antics of a little bird which was hopping from
cross-twig to cross-twig of its wiry cage, and singing merrily, as if to impart a
corresponding mirthfulness in the heart of its fair mistress.   An eastern carpet
covered the floor ; paintings, amorous and religious, adorned the yellow coloured
walls ; and, like those of the wealthier classes of the day, the ceiling was hid by
silken sheets, so disposed as to represent the ceiling of a Venetian boudoir.   A

small circular table stood beside the couch, whose surface was covered with low
square bottles of rich wines and inspiring waters, for the reinvigorating of the
feeble frame of the invalid.   But these were untouched, while an earthen jar
of water beside them was more than half emptied.   The costume of the orange
girl was composed of a simple tight-fitting frock of green velvet ; a pointed collar
of worked lace, and a string of pearls around her waist.   A small golden cross
hung from her neck by a blue ribbon, and lay on her breast ; a bracelet of hair,
    No. 11.

mounted with gold, encircled her left wrist, and a plain ring adorned her fore-finger. Her hair was in clusters, and fell in profusion over her alabaster neck. Her feet, scarcely perceptible, were encased in slippers of green morocco, and adorned with small square silver buckles. In fine, the apartment resembled more the boudoir of some gay and coquettish belle than that of a poor deluded girl; and the fair occupant herself some spoiled, effeminate child of titled parents, than the daughter of a poor and obscure fruit vender.

But these things aside.

A low knock at the door broke the reflective train of the orange girl's thoughts "Come in," was the response, in a low, soft voice.

The door opened, and a lady of imperial dress and beauty entered the chamber.

"How art thou, love?" said the latter, in a tone of affectionate anxiety.

"Better, much better," replied the orange girl, faintly; "a few days more, and I shall cease to trouble earth."

"Nay, Eugenie," rejoined her companion, playfully, "we'll have no such melancholy sentiment as that born in our palace household. We brought thee here to make thee happy and life-loving, and we shall not suffer thee to harbour any thought traitorous to our intentions or to happiness. Life was given us to enjoy, not to cause us misery; and it is impiety to be wretched, when we can be happy. Thou must live for thine own sake, for ours, and for love's."

"Love's? Ah, your highness!"

"Highness! Hey-day! Mine own loved friend and companion growing cold and distant! Highness me not, Eugenie; I am no highness to thee. To thee now, as ever, I am plain Isabel. I love thee with a sister's love, and thou, loving me the same, must call me, as heretofore, 'dear Isabel.' Because bride to the doge, am I to lose the affectionate greetings of my friends? Marry, not I! Friendship and love are too rare to be sacrificed so cheaply. Call me Isabel, dear Isabel, or never word speak to me again.

"Dear Isabel."

"There's a dear girl," said the other, kissing her, and twining her arms around the orange girl's neck, "thus shalt thou call me ever. As for title, art thou not the greater highness of the two? Did not the patriots, in token of thy wrongs, use thy well known nickname as their signal cry, their watchword, to inspire each other with confidence and courage in their brave enterprise! By my troth! I shall henceforth 'highness' thee, in revenge, if thou darest title me again. But I've a word for thee. Now, don't blush, but boldly guess what it is!"

"Nay, I cannot guess."

"Cannot guess—my sister, Eugenie, cannot guess! Oh, horrid! Thou a woman, and cannot guess? Shocking! I shall henceforth deem thee other than thou art, if thou can'st not guess! Look in my eyes!"

"I see nothing but love, dear Isabel!"

"Nothing but love! Of course not! Galliano always says the same: and kisses my lips as a punishment for every such assertion. Nothing but lov M-ry! I want thee to see nothing else in them! But there are other eyes could look even more fondly on thee than mine; and my dear sister must let them do so. Come, promise me that they shall have such permission!"

"Dear Isabel——"

"Nay, nay, no treachery, my pretty little captive. Like a grim and hideous bear, I'll hug thee into consenting. Dost thou refuse? Nay, then, thus I keep my word!" And she clasped the orange girl affectionately to her breast.

Eugenie wept.

"Nay, pretty trembler," said her companion, in the same mock-serious tone, "have I not already told thee that tears, and all other symptoms of unhappiness, are treachery to our court! The edict has gone forth—'No tears here!' and wilt thou be the first to be summoned to judgment? Come—come, my little rebel, we'll have no tears—this is the palace of the graces, Love, Hope, and Happiness! See that thou rememberest it!"

"Even for joy, dear Isabel, I should weep."

"Tears are traitors to joy, sweet one. Put on thy smiles, thy brightest ones, for there is a certain young lieutenant—whilom a gondolier—who desires speech with thee. He is in the ante-chamber, fretting his life away, lest his fair mistress should refuse to accept him for her tyrant. I am his ambassador to the court of love, and the queen of that heart-breaking court must not refuse to reward him for his fidelity."

A tear now danced in the earnest eye of Eugenie.

"Shall I bid him enter?" said the duchess, in a tone, half playful, half earnest.

"Oh, spare me—spare him! I am unfit to wed!" exclaimed the orange girl in reply.

"Unfit to wed! Now, by St. Mark! thou art the very image of a simple-witted child! Unfit to wed! Art thou not ringed and widowed—art thou not free and loving? Was life given thee to make a mockery of? Are thy friends blind to thy merits or thy virtues? Hast thou no virtues? If ay, shouldst thou not give them to the eyes of the world, that they may be taken note of and acknow-ledged? Shalt thou for a paltry squeam refuse to live out thy appointed time as happily as possible? Wilt thou be thine own foe? Be wise—thy lover adores thee, loves thy very footprints, and would sacrifice his life's dearest hopes to make thee happy, to call thee his. And wilt thou do him such deep wrong as to let such devotion as his go unrewarded, unrequited? Go to! Foscari did thee wrong, but righted thee at last; thou art his widow now,—in sight of heaven and earth, his widowed bride! Heaven and earth so look upon thee; and so thou art, let who will gainsay it! The doge of Venice, the duchess, the whole court, ay, and every honest mind in Venice, will vouch the same against any caviller soever! Wrong not thyself by flinging aside the honest heart and brave hand of him who hath ever loved thee dearer than himself."

Eugenie still wept, and the glow of conscious shame shone on her cheeks. She reflected, and she wept while she reflected.

"Summon thy courage at once," said the duchess affectionately, "and bid me call him in."

The eyes of the orange girl and those of her friend met—it was a meaning glance—the next moment Eugenie was alone.

Her eye grew calm on the instant—no gush of blood marred the alabaster hue of her brow or cheek. Her lip was pale, but firm. A light tread caught her ear—the door opened, and Gennaro, now a lieutenant in the body guard of the doge, was at her feet.

They were alone.

She did not bid him rise; but there was a language in her eyes which Gennaro, novice as he was in love's ambiguous tongue, understood at once.

He sat by her side—her hand in his—his arm around her waist—her head bowed on his breast.

Need we tell their speech, as thus they sat? No; there are scenes and whispers free from the profane pen of the scribe.

The day following, whispers were heard in the palace of a bridal—a private bridal,—at which the doge enacted the father's part, and gave away the bride. The duchess also had a part in the matter; and so did the lady of the duke's secretary. There were some tears shed before, during, and after the ceremony; but on such occasions women have a right to weep—though we cannot tell for what.

Years passed on, and a group of little boys were assembled in the private garden of the ducal palace. They were a merry little group, and were wrestling for a wreath which a lovely girl, in the simple costume of an orange vendor, who stood in the centre of a green plat, held in her hand. A young fellow, about twelve years of age, who called himself her little husband, won the prize, and, like a true little knight, knelt at the feet of the little beauty, while she placed it, gracefully, amid the shouts of the little party, upon his brow,

A party of ladies and gentlemen were sitting on cushioned benches in the balcony gazing with affectionate anxiety on the scene. There was a shade or two of deeper age upon their brows and faces than when we saw them last; but they were gently touched by Time, for all that; and they all looked so happy too!

Shall we tell their names? Well, Galliano, the doge, and Isabel, the duchess; Gennaro, the leader of the Venetian forces, and Eugenie, his beloved; Calvari, now secretary of state, and his talkative and merry-hearted Junetta; Paulo, captain of the doge's body-guard, and a little body, that he had caught in a house where mourning was, because its head had been decapitated in consequence of being one of the "Ten;" he had caught her there, we say, and in his efforts to console her for her father's loss, somehow or other got her to accept him as her protector for the remainder of her natural life. Young men have such ways with them!

The reign of the doge Galliano was one of prosperity and happiness to Venice; and to this day, old gossips and young lovers cajole old time by the recital of the events caused by the wrongs of the Orange Girl of Venice.

THE END.